BYSTANDER

a novella

By

Jacqui Jacoby

BODY COUNT
PRODUCTIONS, INC.

Library of Congress: 2015913843

ISBN, print: 978-0-9966157-5-4

ISBN, e-book: 978-0-9966157-6-1

First Edition, 2015.

www.bodycountproductionsinc.com

DEDICATION

To my continuing source of amusement, entertainment

and never ending supply of affection…

Connor, Murphy,

Quincy, Hudson,

and Gomez.

ACKNOWLEDGEMENTS

Larry Wilson

Scene Idea Consultant

Caroline Dunsheath & Trisha Leazier Wilson

Editing by Nas Dean

nas_dean@ymail.com

Cover Design

by

Bridgette Wilson with additional services by Angie Waters

CHAPTER ONE

Sean Branigan downshifted as he hit the light, his Audi R8 Sport sliding to a stop he didn't want to be at. The GPS was set to Miles Criswell's condo, but it wasn't Miles Criswell he wanted to see.

He looked at his watch, noting twenty-two minutes had passed since he'd received the text from Beth Hardwick. Apparently, Beth wasn't having all too good a night and calling Sean was her only recourse.

He turned off the radio's rendition of a *Jingle Bells* commercial even though it was only four days until Thanksgiving and pulled up at the place the GPS said, parking next to a fire hydrant at eleven o'clock at night, facing the opposite way. It was the only available spot and with the nerves he carried, he figured he would fuck a ticket or a tow.

She was in trouble.

Getting out, he reached Number 15 at the same time Allonzo arrived. It wasn't a bad idea to bring your six-four-and-a-half, two-hundred-twenty-five-pound, special-op trained security guard to a black op rescue mission.

Sean looked at his watch again.

"She called twenty-seven minutes ago."

"What did she say?" Allonzo asked.

"Sorry," Branigan said squeezing his eyes tight. "She texted. There's trouble."

"And boss man wants to play superhero, huh?" The smile cracking the dark face was more annoying than infuriating.

"Do I pay you extra for unnecessary sarcasm or is it included?"

Allonzo smiled. "Number 15. Right there."

Branigan walked up the mildly overgrown walkway while Allonzo stayed a little way back.

Sean knew both Miles and Beth. Both worked for him, both were great people, but the kiss Branigan had been dying for from Beth for months, should have waited. Today was too soon.

Sean knocked on the door, heard several muffled words, a loud *shhh* and then a 'get the fuck back'.

The door pulled open and Miles, beer in hand, leaned against the jamb. Judging by the look on his face now, he wasn't the good guy Sean had thought him to be.

"What do you want? It's after hours."

"Yeah, I know," Sean said. "We were heading over to get a drink and thought you might like to join us. Guys night out."

"Who is he?" He motioned with his beer.

"Oh him? That's Allonzo. You've seen him around."

"Who the fuck is Allonzo?"

"You know the studio. Slapping security on for no reason. He gets thirsty, too. Why are all the lights out?"

"Saving energy."

"Where's Beth?"

Miles leaned on the doorjamb. "She doesn't live here anymore."

"Go, run," an urgent, breathless voice called. "You need to go. He's got a gun."

"I think maybe she does." Sean looked over his shoulder. "Allonzo, can you make sure he doesn't have a gun?"

Allonzo smiled and moved up the walkway. "Sure."

Sean saw Miles go for the weapon, but Allonzo moved faster, getting Miles into a body lock and slamming him against the door before yanking the weapon from Miles' hand.

"It's a .45," Allonzo said, "but it doesn't feel full enough."

Sean walked past the two into the living room. Even with the shadows, he could see her curled up on the end of the couch. He walked over to the end table, turning on the light, tilting his chin as he looked down at her.

She looked away, not meeting his gaze. Her thick, long blonde hair was a mess, her make-up smeared. The dress she was wearing this afternoon torn at the sleeve. With her legs pulled up, it rode high on her thighs, but she didn't seem to notice. The tears were only partially dry on her bruised face.

He put a finger under her chin and pulled her face forward so he could see the deep hand prints on one cheek before pushing away to see the ones on the other side.

He knelt in front of her.

"He was in the warehouse," she said softly

"I kinda figured that out," he said.

"He heard what you said."

"What did I say?"

"About being jealous. He wanted to show you what jealousy looked like."

He tried to smile but guilt edged his gut. "I've actually seen jealousy before and it doesn't look anything like this."

She smiled a little but it was strained.

"When you sent the text, did you call the police?"

"I didn't send the text."

He thought with pursed lips for a moment, his hands clasped in front of him. "He took your phone?"

"Um…humph," she said.

"He wanted to get me here?"

"Um…humph."

"It's probably a good thing I called Allonzo, then."

"Um…humph."

"What's with you pretty boys?" Miles said from behind him.

"See," he said, smiling up at her. "I would have to disagree with him right there. Never thought of myself that way."

He stood up and started to turn.

"Exotic," he heard her whisper.

He looked down at her. "I like that."

"You have everything you want," Miles said. "The parts, the money, cars, super models in your bed. Why the fuck do you have to come sniffing around my average piece of shit?"

Sean blinked and pursed his lips again. "Average piece of shit? You call her nice names like that and it might explain why it was so fucking easy to get her to look twice."

Miles made a move and Allonzo slammed him against the door.

"You want to call off your dog and really discuss this?"

"No," Sean said. "Nothing to prove."

"Check her phone," Miles snapped.

"Where is it?" Sean asked.

"My back pocket."

Allonzo retrieved it and tossed it to Sean.

"Don't," she said leaning forward, grabbing Sean's arm.

"Why not?" Sean asked.

"You walked right into it," Miles said. "She's been a fan for years. Watched all the movies. You could have done her right there in the warehouse. She's always been hot for you."

"I haven't done a film in twelve years and I made them so people could watch them, genius."

"Look at the phone. She's got your picture all over it."

"I've got pictures of you on my phone," Sean said. "We took them at the picnic."

"Not like these. These are movie and promo photos, showing you off."

"I'm kinda flattered."

"That's not fair," she said, leaning forward. "It's the book. Remember I told you I was doing this book?"

"Yeah," Sean said. "I remember."

"The character. He's with the CIA. I was working on him and he reminded me of you. I mean, not you, but like you. I have tons of photos on my phone for stories. Puppies and weapons and clothes and characters. I have Orlando Bloom, too."

"Now I'm really flattered. Allonzo, call 911."

He knelt down and picked up her hands, turning them palm up.

He raised her wrists toward her. "And these?"

She looked away, tearing up. He squeezed her hands a little.

"Allonzo, the cops will be here in a few. Do you think you can hurt him bad without leaving a mark so we all can deny it when he accuses us?"

"Sure," Allonzo said, smiling.

Sean smiled. "Hurt him."

He looked back at her.

"I'm sorry, Beth. This wasn't what I intended."

"I know." She smiled a little. She looked down, her color about as off as her breathing.

"You have stuff here?"

She looked to her lap and picked at her fingernails.

"Beth," he said, his voice soft. "You came back because you left some stuff?"

"He wasn't going to do it," she said softly.

"Do what?"

She looked at him and shook her head. "He would not have done it."

"Okay," Sean said, holding her hand. "You said you had stuff here?"

"A couple pairs of earrings. A book I didn't finish. I forgot my favorite shoes in the closet. The red ones. I could have lived without all of those and none of this would've happened."

"Beth, this isn't your fault. You know that."

She jumped from the couch, shocking him. By the time he reached the bathroom, the door had slammed shut and he could hear her through the wood—being sick.

His face screwing up, he put a clenched fist against the door and breathed in and out as deep as he could.

"Allonzo," he called through the small condo.

"Yep," the deep voice replied.

"Hurt him bad." A few minutes later, Allonzo pulled Sean away from his post.

Sean left the bathroom door and came into the living room where a police officer stood looking tough and perplexed.

Miles was outside the door in Allonzo's cuffs muttering and spewing about lawsuits and pain.

"He says you hurt him," the cop said.

"Does he have any marks?" Allonzo asked, showing his security credentials.

"I'm thinking it wouldn't be an issue with you." The lady cop turned to Sean. "And I heard you say hurt him."

The bathroom door opened and Beth wandered out looking dazed, her eyes downcast.

Sean shifted his attention from the police to her.

"Which I think I didn't really hear," the cop said. "He did that?"

"And he had the gun I put in the freezer," Allonzo said. "The two rounds it had in it is on the counter."

Sean helped Beth to the couch, his arm under her elbow while the officer called for an ambulance.

The cop knelt in front of Beth.

"Can I have your name," the officer asked.

Allonzo came over and put a blanket over Beth's shoulders.

"Beth," she said. "Beth Hardwick."

"I'm Officer Linda Bezinover. Can you tell me what happened?"

"Miles goes out on Tuesdays. He and his friends shoot pool over at Arnolds on Ventura Blvd. I used to stay here and forgot a few things when I left so I thought I could grab them and go."

"You have a key?"

"Did. He took it."

"And how did this happen?"

She looked at the floor. "I don't really know. He was here when I didn't know it. He popped out. Then he was yelling, accusing me of things and then he wasn't yelling. He took my phone and texted Mr. Branigan."

"Do you know why?"

"I guess he wanted him here since he was the one Miles was accusing me of cheating on him with."

The officer looked at Sean. "With reason?"

"Potential, not official yet. Definitely not enough to account for this brutality."

The officer looked at Sean. "Can you give us a minute please?"

"Of course."

Sean backed away with Allonzo until they were out of earshot.

The men stared at each other, neither one bringing up the questions of rape now presented. Sean closed his eyes and thought if she said yes, he wouldn't need Allonzo to break Miles apart.

The ambulance arrived without sirens and a stretcher was brought in.

Sean, Allonzo and Officer Bezinover stepped back while the EMT's took care of Beth.

"And who are you?" Bezinover asked.

He looked at her.

"Okay, I know who you are. Who are you to this case?"

"New boyfriend. Criswell and Beth broke up. He caught us being friendly and lost a socket."

"How friendly?"

"Couple of kisses. That's it. I received a text from her there was trouble and when I came here, she said he sent the message to lure me. No confession on what the plans were but I'm thinking they weren't good."

"What about him?" She asked.

Sean looked at Allonzo then back to Officer Bezinover. "I get a midnight call for help and I'm bringing back-up. It's why I employ it."

She looked at him. "Why not just send the back-up? Someone like you doesn't need to get dirty in this."

"Someone like me? You mean a man with a kickass girlfriend he wants safe? Good to know you enjoyed the movies."

She stared at him and didn't comment as Beth came out on the stretcher and was loaded in the van.

"Can I ride?" He asked the EMT.

"And you are?"

"The boyfriend who didn't do this."

"Okay. We'll be ready in a minute."

Sean nodded and turned to Allonzo. He rubbed his palm over his eyes. "Can you get some help and get my car to the hospital?"

"Of course." Allonzo took the keys.

"And get whatever she was after. She said earrings, shoes, a book."

"I'll look around. There might be something that says her."

"Susan's house. Have Susan help you get all her stuff. Take it to my place. Adian is there alone anyway. I didn't mind a couple of hours but this might go all night."

"I'll take care of it."

Sean almost smiled up at Allonzo. "You know most of this shit is above and beyond."

"And most bosses aren't worth shit. I'll take care of it. You take care of her. And yourself. You look a little thrashed."

Sean raised his eyebrows and tilted his chin. "Yeah."

"We're ready," the EMT called and Sean turned, climbing into the ambulance to sit out of the way. He could see Beth with the O2 tube on her face. Her eyes closed, her fingers clenched, the marks on her face standing out stark against her pale skin.

He waited a few minutes in silence, looking for a sign of life, but she didn't move.

"Hey," Sean said. "Beth?"

She didn't respond. The EMT raised her gaze to his.

He smiled. "Is it okay?" he asked.

She nodded.

"Beth, which movies did you like? I heard you liked the movies. Which ones?"

The EMT grinned a little and looked down.

Beth didn't answer right away. He could see her jaw working. He wanted to get her to talk. He wanted to get her thinking about something else.

"I can tell you which was the most fun to make."

She pulled the mask down. *"Daily Grind,"* she said, her voice soft.

He chuckled. "How did you know that?"

"Could tell. Whole cast. You guys had blast on that set. Made the movie fun to watch."

"We did. What about you? Which one did you like?"

She took a deep breath. Then another. Then another.

"Days Gone Bad."

He chuckled. "I don't hear that one often. That's kinda cool."

She hadn't opened her eyes. Her fingers were still clenched.

"The part was good," she said. "The lover who shouldn't have been a lover. Very well played. His devastation at her murder was…" she searched for a word. "Heart-wrenching, though I didn't like the suicide ending but I think he lost too much already. He couldn't do it alone anymore. Maybe they got another chance."

He was impressed.

"I hated *Mortal Sin.*"

He smiled and nodded, liking that she was comfortable enough with him even now to call him out on it. Her fingers weren't as tight. "Why is that?"

"Shallow. The character didn't have depth. He grieved his wife's death and then he basically had grief of his wife's death. Even years later. The heroine was in no way a heroine. She was conniving and manipulative from the start, getting him to dinner, getting him into bed, making him think it was his idea. I was glad when it was over. I never watched it again. I saw *Days Gone Bad* four times."

"Reviews on *Mortal Sin* were bad, too."

"I know. They should have been. I almost got a kitten after I saw *Days Gone Bad.* I wanted to name it James Kelly. I thought that would be a perfect name for a kitten."

She opened her eyes and shifted so she could see him.

She wanted to name a kitten after his character in a movie almost no one saw. But she saw it. Four times. "You like cats?"

"Um…hum. I love cats. I just can't have one now. Maybe later."

"Maybe later," he smiled.

The ambulance parked, and she was wheeled away while he was told to wait and would be called.

CHAPTER TWO

He moved through the ER, grateful for the few people. The decorations up for Thanksgiving consisted of a turkey and some falls leaves but they didn't bring any positive mood to the stark white room. It looked like a hospital and it smelled like a hospital and there was not much to be done about it.

Going to the registration desk, he chewed on the remnants of his patience as he watched the distracted woman behind the glass. After waiting in vain for some response, he finally tapped on the glass.

Her gaze came up and her expression froze for a second.

She slid the partition. "You're Sean Branigan."

"Yes, I am. And I have a friend who was brought in. I wanted to see if I could make some arrangements about it."

"Oh my God," she squealed. "Kasi," she looked over her shoulder to the dark woman in the flowered uniform. "Come here."

He didn't want to deal with Kasi any more than he wanted to deal with her.

"Wow," Kasi said. "I know the area is hot for celebrities but we don't see them very often."

"That's a good thing," he said. "We like to avoid ERs. My friend?"

"Does this friend have a name?"

"Beth Hardwick."

"Girlfriend?"

"Excuse me," he said. They actually shocked him with the question. This wasn't the time nor the place.

"Google said you are seeing Meghan Hartly, not a Beth Hardwick and Meghan is not bad to be thinking about."

"I actually don't give a fuck what Google says. I want to make arrangements for Beth."

A little put off, the receptionist put together a packet on a clipboard.

"I want to get her into a private room, even in the ER so we can avoid shit like this and have some privacy. And if they're keeping her overnight, the same. I'll be staying."

"What is Lekon Sesay like?" Kasi asked. "Was he as funny on the set?"

Lekan Sesay, his co-star in *Long Odds*.

"He's a moron who can't remember his lines."

Lekan wasn't, of course. He was a really nice guy, but Sean's patience was gone.

"I need this filled out," she said, handing him the stack. "The top sheet needs to be signed and I need her insurance information. We don't usually do private rooms in the ER. You understand." She smiled.

"Do you know you're a groupie or am I the first one to tell you?"

Bitch.

Her face fell. "What?"

He stared at the top sheet that needed signing. It was a fucking blank piece of paper.

He grabbed a pen, leaned onto the counter with the clipboard, signing his name across the page. He added a phone number.

"Call this number tomorrow and ask for Mack. Tell her Uncle Scrooge gave you two passes on set for a day visit."

"What?" she beamed.

He handed back the entire stack without filling out anything. He pulled out his wallet and slapped his Visa onto the counter.

"Fuck insurance and cover any expenses with this. Get me that private room, get me back there now or I will make one phone call, turning this place into a media circus for a week, shutting this ER down and listing both of you as the most insensitive, greedy autograph hounds I've ever met."

The clocked edged toward two, Sean sat in the corner, his legs stretched out and his hands resting on his middle. He could be asleep from what she could see. No talking, no movement and a clock registering way too late.

Him—here—was a concept she was having trouble wrapping her head around.

For the last couple of months he had been in the prop rooms a lot more than any of his scripts required. Though he seemed interested in everyone, he always ended up around her, getting her coffee, sitting to talk stories in her office.

She liked those times. And after she was able to get comfortable with a man she watched onscreen, she found she liked him more than she should.

There were a lot of questions. About her life, her job, the writing she did on the side. He never asked her about Miles and she liked that, liked that he didn't want to know.

Because by the time Mr. Branigan—Sean, he wanted her to call him Sean—had really settled into one of their thinking chairs in the room, she already had started to question Miles herself. He was a mistake she didn't know how to walk away from.

Charming to a fault, willing to do just about anything to please, he would drop a wad of cash on dinner then make you feel like he did you a favor while he smiled.

She was at the condo for a couple of days and even that had seemed wrong. Four days ago, she called it quits and took a room in Susan's house for a little while. It was small, but nice and Susan was fun to be around.

Beth hadn't realized how twisted Miles was, but what Miles had planned to do to Sean, would have made the papers in the morning.

Mr. Branigan was Hollywood royalty. Writer and producer of his hit show *Snap Shots*, he was the child of the previous Hollywood royalty. Both his folks were stars in their own right in the sixties and seventies. With two brothers, both working in the industry, Sean made his films then took his Masters from UCLA and started writing scripts.

Tall, dark and handsome just about covered it. He kept his hair long, his face was above average with that exotic hint. His intense, deep blue eyes stared down from more than one teenage girl's wall.

At precisely 3:42 this afternoon—she knew because she had just looked at her watch—he joined her in the prop room, pulling the door shut behind him. He spoke for a minute or two then asked her if he could test a theory.

"Close your eyes," he said. "And don't jump."

And then he kissed her. *Sean Branigan* had *kissed her*.

Not just once either. A few times, testing new angles and new techniques, though each of his techniques was about as good as the rest of him. His hand on her lower back, the other fisted in her hair, he took her high so fast the air got thin.

Looking at him asleep in the chair the experience was still surreal.

Just four days out and away from Miles, she didn't know where to file it.

"How long are you planning on staring?" he asked when he hadn't opened his eyes to check.

Tonight was a nightmare she didn't want to carry, yet she smiled a little at the comment.

"I wasn't staring."

"Grow up in my house and you know when people are staring. You've known me for five years. There's nothing to see."

"Our circumstances were a little different before."

His closed mouth smile with those closed eyes was wicked. "Yes. Yes, they were."

"You can go home," she said.

"Why would I want to do that?" he asked.

"You have a son at home. Maybe the parent stuff."

"He's thirteen and can handle one night." He looked at his watch. "Besides the nurse said it would only be a few more minutes."

"Why did you do it? You didn't have to do that."

"Needed to find out," he replied.

"Find out what?"

He smiled then. "I had been working on this theory for weeks but hadn't had a chance to act on it."

"Where's Meghan?"

He opened his eyes and shifted his chin to look at her. "She left. About a week ago."

"You two weren't still—"

He shook his head slow. "Not for a while actually, though we went through the motions. Less questions that way."

"But—"

"But what? I had no attachments when I walked in that prop room."

"But Miles?"

"Miles and you broke up four weeks ago, you just didn't get the memo. The fact you waited until four—" he looked at his watch again. "—five days ago to act is a miracle. There was a poll on set about how long it would take you to realize it."

"What?" she half laughed. "That's stupid."

His gaze came up to hers.

She leaned forward, out of breath. "But why are you here?"

"It's where my car is. Makes sense I would follow my car."

She leaned back in frustration and let out a heavy sigh as she melted into the pillow.

He raised his brows. Laughed and leaned forward. "The company picnic. Remember?"

"Yeah, seven, eight weeks back."

"You and I, there with respective partners. We didn't really had a conversation before and we get hooked up in almost every game they tossed at us. Remember?"

She nodded.

"Potato sack first, some karaoke duets, a little water ballooning. You got that henna tattoo on your shoulder."

"Yes. I remember."

"The potato race was luck of the draw. Every time we were hooked after that, it was me begging, pleading and paying whoever was in charge of the game."

"What?" her voice was breathless.

"I had you in my arms in that race. I had never done that with you, never been that close, and I fucking never had any woman reduce me to blubber by a whiff of her mere shampoo. And your fucking laugh," he said with a smile. "I was toast in one leg of the track." He leaned back, grinning. "Then you went about your business ignoring me for eight weeks."

"I kinda work for you. I'm supposed to ignore you."

"You work for the show, while I don't so we are under no obligation to play nice because of it. But you were still with Miles and I was with Meghan so I had to wait. In the last couple of days I really did think it was just a formality with you two and moved forward before I should."

"That's why you're here. You feel guilty about this."

"Well yes, that's true, but it's not why I'm here."

"I don't understand."

He leaned back and closed his eyes.

His smile broadened. "I figured a while ago, once you got away from him then you and I could start the long term relationship I'm planning on. The house is in the Hollywood Hills on Freemont. Great view of the city."

"What house?" she asked with less confidence than she wanted to portray. He didn't say what he just said.

His eyes opened, gaze shifting to hers and he grinned.

"You are serious."

"Yes," he said.

She leaned forward a little and motioned to her face with both hands. "Forget this is even here and make believe tonight never happened. There is still no way in hell."

"Why is that?"

"Because the world pretty much knows who you are dating and when, and I don't fall into any category which measures up to your usual taste."

"Why is that?"

"I'm too short, not thin enough and my boobs are not only home-grown, they are way too small. You like super models, and are one of the few men who can get them out of a catalog. Not an area I know a lot about."

He closed his eyes again and leaned back. "It's been a fucked up night, it's almost three and you are probably carrying some insecurities right now, all of which I plan on helping with. We can talk more tomorrow after we get up. Maybe a good breakfast. I can make a good breakfast."

"I'm going to Susan's house. Tomorrow I have to get my stuff."

"Not in my car."

"I didn't expect you to drive me."

"Expect it."

"To Susan's?"

"No, as soon as we are done here we're going to my house. A lot of protection there, a lot of safety and you might just go to sleep with that hug you need tonight."

"You're kidnapping me?"

He smiled again and she wished he would stop. "I'm executing a rescue mission."

CHAPTER THREE

He got to the front door, key in hand and stopped, pausing as he looked at her.

"You said you liked cats."

"What?"

"You like cats?"

She tilted her chin "I love cats."

He smiled silly. "Good to hear it."

He turned the key, letting them in and right smack in front of them was a mammoth grey stretching out in the foyer as if he owned the place. He had to be over fifteen pounds. By the entrance to the next room, was an orange, much smaller. Sitting, staring and blinking in an accusatory way.

Sean pointed. "That's Raphael, by the door. This lazy ass here is Donatello."

She leaned over to pet Donatello's head.

"He doesn't like when we leave," Sean said. "So he blocks the entrance when we come home."

Donnie purred and batted at her fingers. "Leonardo and Michelangelo are in there somewhere, probably doing something they shouldn't be."

"You have four cats?"

He stopped and looked at her. "Yeah. Problem?"

"Named after The Ninja Turtles?"

"No. Renaissance painters."

"You have a thirteen-year-old son and you think I'm going to buy your turtle cats are named after painters?"

He smiled. "It was worth a try."

"Why am I here?"

"It's where my car is," he said again, smiling. "Makes sense I'm with my car and you're with me."

Her gaze stayed more toward the floor.

All the lights were on.

Allonzo sat on the couch, reading a book.

"He's supposed to be asleep."

"You tell him that," Allonzo said.

"I was worried," a voice came from the kitchen area.

A kid came out, looking pretty much like the unmatured version of the man she was with all night. She turned away to hide her face.

"Don't worry about it, Beth. It's cool," he said, smiling and not staring. "But he's in jail, right?"

"Why are you up?" Sean asked with his annoyed 'dad' voice. "Why is he up?" he asked Allonzo. "He has school in five hours."

"I'm not going today," the kid beamed, then turned to walk in the other direction. "I made a pot of tea about an hour ago. It's probably not hot since no one called to let me know when you were coming home."

"You were supposed to be asleep when I knew I would be late."

Sean looked at her. "You think I'm difficult to deal with, try taking him on."

"I'm going to take off," Allonzo said. "Set the alarms and lock the doors. Beth if you have any problems, call me direct. My number's in your phone. I put it there."

"Thank you," she whispered.

"I made brownies, too," Adian said. "You know for the whole cheer up angle."

"Adian," Sean said in a stern voice.

"Dad," the kid smiled back. When Sean glared at him, Adian handed him a brownie.

Sean mumbled under his breath. "Fucking, son-of-a-bitch. Every time. Every *single* time." He bit into his brownie.

"Come on in," Adian said. "How big dad is on manners depends on how big their boobs are when they walk in the door."

Beth laughed for the first time since the horror. The kid was too cute not to.

Sean swore off another curse. "I swear, you are grounded until you are twenty-five."

"Come on. Time for bed."

She wished he hadn't used that expression. She and Adian were discussing movies not starring his dad while drinking warmed tea.

"Thank you, Adian," she said and she got a smile back.

"Go to bed," Sean said as he walked her across the kitchen to a hallway leading toward the city views.

As a master, it did master, she thought looking at the furniture from the doorway. The bed—pristine in its black and white sheets and bedding, a door that probably led to a bathroom. She assumed it had a tub big enough to float a boat. His closet door stood ajar, that was straight with lines leading back making her think it might be big enough to subdivide.

The view in the full window showed city lights on a dark night.

She stood, staring at it all, wondering when Rod Serling would be coming in.

He stood behind her.

"Humph," she mumbled.

"What?" he asked.

She looked over her shoulder at him. "That's a nice bed. A king."

"Yeah," he said.

She smiled shyly.

"Is this where Meghan slept when she was here?" She turned to look at him.

He smiled. "Meghan kept her own place, but yeah, there were some nights she stayed here."

"You stayed there?"

He shook his head. "Not all night. I really don't like leaving Adian alone."

"We're on what? Season five?"

"Okay, yes," he laughed. "In five seasons there may have been a couple of overnight guests."

"Where were you planning on sleeping?"

He nodded and chuckled. "I actually planned on sleeping in my bed."

She walked forward to pick up the throw at the base and moved to pick up a pillow.

She looked at him.

"It's more tempting then you know to kiss that expression off your face."

29

"The couch is fine," she said. "I need to get out of your hair early anyway."

He took her by the hand. Walking slightly stiff with annoyance, he moved down the hall to another door, pushing it open. He let her go in first.

She stood at the end of the queen size bed, then looked to him.

"My mother's room. She stays here when she comes to town and I seriously doubt there have been any improprieties in this bed. And if there have, I so don't want to hear about them."

"Your mother?"

"Yeah, she lives in Carmel. Comes down to see Adian every couple of months. "

She walked around the bed and sat on its edge, bouncing up and down a bit. She looked at him.

"It's nice. And no cooties."

"Cooties?"

"You call it what you want. I'll call it what I want."

"It's also four in the morning. You have some time off work and I will take what I can. All your stuff from Susan's is in the living room."

"My pajamas?"

"If you had pajamas, then yes. I can get those for you if you don't mind me pawing your stuff."

"I can put all those in a hotel."

He looked around the room at the dresser and vanity. "No one uses this room."

She stood up, dropping her shoulders and sighed.

"He likes you," he said,

"Who?"

"Adian. He told me weeks ago. And he didn't like Meghan which is an indication right off the bat I wouldn't be in that relationship for too long. Either he approves or you're out. You, he *pre*-approved."

He walked over to the computer, pulled up an email and typed quickly.

He grinned and stood up.

"That's one problem solved."

"What did you do?"

He looked at the computer and back at her. "I emailed my PA to get a new bed in my room by tomorrow afternoon, complete with all new sheets, washed with Downy."

"You wield a lot of power over people."

"I have a lot of money and a name people think is cool. I always thought it was kind of, I don't know, weird. Too much notoriety, but I was stuck with it, and it comes in handy on nights I need to use it. Like when a houseguest insists on purified mattresses."

He smiled again. "We can have this discussion tomorrow."

"I won't be here tomorrow," she said.

"Security is set. Open a door and…" he grinned and shrugged dramatically.

It was closer to five when he went out in the hall outside her room. He could hear her moving around inside. When the closet doors shut and the drawers started opening and closing, he knocked.

"Beth," he said softly.

"I'm okay," he heard through the door.

He took a chance and opened it a few inches. A cat ran in.

He could see her standing in the middle of the room, her arms around herself.

"Are you okay?"

She swung around to look at him.

"Are you looking for something?"

She looked at the dresser and back. "I'm sorry, I wasn't prying."

"May I come in?" he asked.

She nodded.

"I don't care if you are prying or not. It's Mom's shit anyway." He smiled. "If you want, we can go and post it all on eBay and make a profit."

She smiled a little, but it had to hurt.

"How do I help you?" he asked.

"I think you already have."

"Right now. What can I do for you right now, besides exploit my mom?"

She smiled again. "But I think you've done enough for me."

"I would like to do more."

She looked down and backed away.

"Beth?" he asked softly.

"I don't want to be alone," she said, still not looking at him. "It's scary when I am alone."

He nodded toward the bed. "Won't you think the bed gets cooties if I stay?"

Again the almost smile. "Not if you behave."

He walked around to one side of the bed, adjusting the pillow for himself and pulling back the blankets.

She watched him.

"Come on," he said. "I can play nice. Right now you need a friend. I can do that."

She slid under the sheets.

She was quiet for a moment, her big green eyes blinking. He wasn't touching her, but he suspected she was shaking.

"I'm really scared," she whispered. "All I can think about—"

He put a finger on her lips. "You're safe here and right now we don't need to think about all of that."

"I don't know how to turn it off."

He leaned close, but didn't touch.

"Do you want to…um…I would…if you want…" She looked at the space between them.

He ran a hand over her hair. "No."

Her gaze came up. "It might help me forget."

"I don't want to be the guy you forget with. I want to be the guy you want to be with."

She sighed and pulled away.

"I will hold, cuddle, nuzzle and kiss. But that's it and I hope it's enough. If it's not, we'll get some Ben & Jerry's and Hershey bars and make some popcorn."

She smiled and he liked it.

"What were you doing?" she asked.

"When?"

"I don't even know what he texted you but you got there so fast."

He raised his eyebrows and then settled a little further. "It just said '*Help Me*'. It had the photo which I set to your phone number."

"You had to have walked right out of the door."

"I took a minute to get Adian settled, called Allonzo for your address and had him meet me there."

"Why did you go to the condo?"

"I called Susan. She said you went over. She was worried you hadn't come back or called."

"What were you doing when it came in?"

She smiled as he played with her hair.

"I was in the kitchen with Adian, cutting strawberries. He had the sugar out."

"What?" she smiled.

"Adian and I. We split a pint of strawberries almost every night. He finished cutting them tonight and I think he saved them to go with breakfast. He wants to impress you."

"I was impressed with him a couple of months ago, when he started hanging around my office. He didn't act the way I thought a kid should act."

"How is that?"

"Well, he can talk about anything. And I mean that in a good way. He didn't seem to have an age meter on him and he could adjust, with sincerity, to whoever was around. He likes people. No phone out. No gaming system. He wanted to talk to people."

"He wanted you to talk to him. He was interviewing."

"Please don't make me laugh. My face really hurts."

"Sorry," he said, rubbing the back of his knuckles over the tender skin. "You're still beautiful."

"You were in bed with a super model last week and you can say that?"

"I wasn't, so yes."

"You weren't with Meghan a week ago?"

"Not like that. It ended pretty much the same time it started, months ago. It's…" he sighed and rolled over to stare at the ceiling. He thought for a minute. "It's a pain in the ass when the press gets hold of the break-up and plasters it all over the place like it's fun. You can't go to the store and checkout without seeing a tabloid listing the reasons why she dumped you. So we agreed to play act. We knew it would come out eventually but we held it off for a while."

"It's got to be hard on him."

"It can be." He rolled back over. "So I try to control myself. Roll over."

"What?"

"Roll over."

Moving slowly, she did. When she was settled, he scooted across the bed until his chest pressed up against her back, and his face was in her hair, smelling that shampoo. He took a deep breath and settled until they formed one unit. He was right. She was shaking.

"Do I get extra pay for this?" she asked and he smiled.

"Nope. Freebie."

She settled against him, then picked up his hand, entwining their fingers.

The silence went on long enough to make him think she had fallen asleep.

"Sean?"

"Humph."

"I think there's a cat on my feet."

"It's worse than you think. There's one on mine and I think they hate each other."

CHAPTER FOUR

She woke up, rolled over toward the middle of the bed and found him already awake, watching her.

He gently touched her face. "Man, these came in pretty good."

"They hurt."

"Do you need something for it?"

"I don't know."

He reached across her to the nightstand, getting close enough to smell her lingering perfume, then picked the prescription bottle. He shook one out, took the glass of water from his side and handed it all over.

She took the pill watching him with narrowed eyes. He put the water back and picked up his cell phone.

He speed-dialed while laying on his back on the pillow.

"Mack," he said into the phone.

MacKenzie Riley, his right-hand man.

"I need a make-up kit sent to the house sometime this morning. Can you make it happen?"

There was silence.

"Thanks." He put the phone back.

He rolled over to stare at her.

Sean Branigan. On a pillow. In the same bed.

"I'm not going to sleep with you," he said.

"I actually knew that as I have no intention of putting out."

"But we will be moving into my room tonight, with a uncootied bed, but I'm sorry. No sex. Maybe some cuddling. Definitely some kisses, but no sex."

"You know, I never realized you were insane till now."

He smiled and leaned over, kissing her sweetly on the lips. "Morning," he said, pulling back.

Her phone on the nightstand vibrated and she grabbed it, glancing at it, before putting it down.

"Who was that?"

"Susan," she said. "I didn't come home last night."

"Yeah, probably should have checked in," he said, knowing she wasn't aware her coloring dropped a shade. She also didn't know he had texted Susan from the hospital letting her know he was taking over.

Two minutes later when the next text came in, she looked again. "Mom," she said. "We text every morning."

And Beth was a terrible liar.

She set the phone down, this time sliding over toward him.

"You did want to, didn't you? Sleep with me?"

"Dying to. Just not planning on following through for a while."

The phone vibrated and a slight shake started in her body. She ignored the handset.

"You going to get that?"

"Why not?" she asked. "If it's what you want, why not just do it?"

"Because that's not what I want. I told you. I want a long-term relationship with you, I decided it a while ago. We just have to take our time."

"Time for what?"

"A long-term relationship. I just came out of a not so long one. You just got out of a shorter one a couple of days ago. I'm thinking it would be a good idea to take time to examine where we are now."

"What about Adian? You can't bring a woman in here and expect him to like her."

"Why do you think he was in the prop room so much?"

"Kids like that."

"Yeah, they like the weapons room but he always ended up in your office, didn't he? Asking what I had done next on the show."

"How do you know that?"

"He told me. This was his idea, Beth. Or at least he pointed out the possibilities and suggested I stop hanging around with bimbos." Sean smiled. "He actually used the word 'bimbo'."

She smiled, too.

Until the phone vibrated again. Then her gaze dropped and her breathing went shallow.

The door to the bedroom opened. "You better wash those sheets before Gr'ma gets here. She'll have a fit."

"Ever hear the term knock?" Sean asked.

"I made crepes with the strawberries and cream. And there's coffee and tea. It's not going to stay warm so hurry up."

"You taught him to be bossy?"

"Oscar the Grouch was his favorite Sesame Street character. I think it explains a lot."

She got up and didn't look in the mirror. She picked up her phone and carried it to the kitchen. Putting it on the counter, she accepted the cup of coffee Adian handed her.

"Cream and sugar are on the table, if you need those," he said.

The phone vibrated a fifth time.

Sean's hand slapped down on it faster than hers. She put down the coffee and lunged for it, but he kept it out of her reach until she backed up with a pathetic sigh.

"Please don't," she whispered.

"Uh...huh," he mumbled, tongue in cheek. He read the last five messages, all from Miles.

Where are you?

I want to talk to you bitch

You will answer me

You better not be with him

If you are with him, I will find both of you and cut your fucking hearts out

Sean's solace in this? She had only looked at the first two. She hadn't seen the rest.

"You know, I think he actually planned on killing me last night."

"I know he did," she whispered and he heard the tears.

He turned toward her while Adian watched silently. *He wouldn't do it,* that's what she said when she was close to shock last night. *He couldn't do it.*

"He told me. He told me how. I just couldn't get to the phone to warn you and you walked right in."

"But you tried, didn't you? That's when he did this," he motioned to her face. "He didn't do this to you because he's an asshole. He did this because you tried to interfere and stop him."

"Dad, what happened?"

Her gaze shifted to Adian then back.

"What was I supposed to do?" she tried to laugh. "Let him get away with it? The world needs nice guys. It doesn't need men like him."

"What was he going to do?"

She shook her head and looked at Adian.

"He knows about deranged fans. It's not going to shock him. Might piss him off it came that close because I did walk right in."

Her gaze jumped to his. "I didn't want you to. He took the phone and—"

"And what?"

She was looking down, searching for the words and he was not going to be anything but gentle with her.

"I was tied up until about five minutes before you came in. He thought I would make better bait if I were loose. He *seriously* was not counting on Allonzo."

Sean sank down onto one of the stools. He looked at her bruised wrists.

"Those were a combination? Pinning down and tying up?"

She shook her head. "He never tried. What I told you was true. I haven't lied to you."

"Just omitted and let me believe. What was he going to do?"

She took her time, wrestling with it. Finally with her gaze down, she whispered. "Murder-suicide."

"That doesn't make sense."

She looked up at him, then away.

"Oh, I get it. I murder you, off myself with my kid at home and he stages the whole thing and walks. Who knew about us and yesterday?"

Her gaze snapped to his. "Not many. He didn't want anyone to know you were that good…"

He set the phone down and rubbed his face with both hands. "Connecting us as lovers. He types out bogus note. I could use this on the show," he tried for humor. "Why didn't you tell the police? It might have upped his staying time."

"I didn't want you to know. I thought it would be safer."

"For who?" he snapped.

She looked down and took a step back.

"Shit," he mumbled, rubbing his forehead.

"I did tell the police," she said softly and those were silent tears on her bruised face. "In the hospital. Before you came back to the room. I didn't have any proof so they couldn't proceed past assault. I asked them not to tell you since there wouldn't be charges on it."

"They had him on entrapment," his voice almost raised.

She shook her head. "It was *my* phone, Sean. There is no way to prove I didn't send that text and he just got home before you and I—" she looked down.

"Oh, fuck," he snapped. He got up from the stool and paced away.

It was quiet in the room.

"I wouldn't have set you up, Sean. You have to believe that. *Please* believe that."

"Dad. Stop."

He turned to look at her, terrified now of something other than last night. He never thought of her as fragile, not until this moment.

She wouldn't look at him as she continued to back away slowly.

Adian picked up her coffee and held it toward her. "Do you want some?" he asked. "We have French vanilla creamer."

"I don't have my car," she whispered while looking at the floor. "Can you call me a car and I can go home? You can probably get a car."

Crap, he sighed, rubbing his face. Yeah. He was a gentleman.

"No," he finally said, filing all the new info with the old and classifying under Miles Criswell.

She managed to look up at him. He stepped toward her. She stepped back.

"I do believe you, Beth. I always have. My plans haven't changed about anything we talked since last night or this morning." He took the paper towel Adian offered and very carefully wiped her face dry.

She wouldn't look at him. "I wouldn't have done that to you."

"Honey," he said gently cupping her cheek. "You're so good you wouldn't have done that to *him*."

"The crepes are still ready," Adian said meekly. "We should eat. We won't be hungry and we can think about who to call."

Sean moved with her toward the table.

A cat jumped up in front of her, black, its tail swishing and green eyes blinking. She reached to stroke it and he saw a small smile at the purr.

"That's Leonardo," Sean said as he pulled out his cell phone. He tapped out a message, hit send then put the display in front of her face.

She read it and looked up at him with sad, scared eyes. She still hadn't seen what Miles said. And four more texts came in while they talked.

Sean's text to Allonzo read: *Escalation. My house ASAP*.

"You have your own security force?"

"Not really," he said as he moved to the table. "It's more like an army."

"Beth, do you like extra whipped cream and powder sugar?" Adian asked.

"Where did you learn to make crepes?" she asked, trying to look happy. She did okay.

"I don't know. We just do it sometimes. Dad cooks, too. He's not too bad."

She pulled out a chair as he put her coffee at the table setting and she jumped.

Sean looked into the seat. The orange and white cat looked up, inconvenienced at having to share.

"That's Mikey," Adian said. "You can push him off."

She slid the chair back, picked up her coffee and switched seats, picking one closer to Sean.

"We had a rule growing up in my house," she said softly as she sat down, the emotions still heavy, the fear—hot. "You never move the cat."

Adian laughed and pointed at her. "We have the same rule."

The text messages kept coming.

About one every ten to twenty minutes. Sean didn't tell her what was written and she seemed okay with it after the trauma she had faced.

Criswell's condo had to be terrifying for her. Being knocked around and tied up was bad enough. Hearing the plans and knowing he would carry them out on both of them had to be petrifying. She had known for hours that not only was she going to die, but he was taking Sean with her. Allonzo said the gun was loaded with two rounds.

One for each of them.

The texts ranged from more threats to sweet talk, saying he was sorry. He wanted her to call him. Could they meet?

When hell froze over.

By the time Allonzo arrived, there were over two dozen.

The LA Basin spread before the window in Sean's office. Beth sat on the couch. Her legs pulled up, across from Allonzo, who had a pen and a pad of paper. She had a cup of herbal tea beside her provided by Adian who stood by his dad.

"Do you mind if I record this?"

She shook her head. A small tape recorder appeared on the table between them.

"Can you tell us how this started?"

"I don't know," she said.

"You had a relationship with Criswell."

She looked down, her gaze shifting to the left before coming back to him.

Allonzo looked in that direction and gave a nod to Sean.

Sean spoke. "Why don't you go and play video games for a while?"

"I can't stay?" Adian asked.

"Beth might be more comfortable. I can tell you what you need to know after."

"I hope it's okay, Beth," Adian said. He shut the door on his way out.

"Thank you," she whispered.

"It's not easy to get caught in these things," Allonzo said. "Hurts the brain and drains the soul. But from what I know now there was a hell of a lot more going last night then we thought."

"I don't know if he would have done it," she said.

"You look like he would have done it," Allonzo said.

Sean walked around the table and sat beside her, picking up her hand, their fingers entwined.

"I never had any problem with him. It was an okay relationship. And then about ten days ago I started staying at the condo and he got real weird."

"Weird how? Were there any threats?"

"Not that I can really point to. We've been doing what…" she looked at Sean. "We were doing what you were doing and then I stayed over and it stopped. The first night. He started sleeping on the couch. After that he always wanted to know what I was doing, where I was."

Allonzo tilted his chin and looked at her.

"What's up?" Sean asked.

"Do you know if he was seeing anyone else?"

She shrugged. "Susan told me after I left it was possible. I didn't know before."

"What?" Sean asked, his voice more sharp.

"There's this concept," Allonzo said. "Fairly misunderstood. It's called a Madonna/Whore complex. Early formed, generally shows up after marriage. A man puts his woman on a pedestal and becomes unable to perform because of her purity. It's not uncommon to stray for sex. He can't get it at home because his wife is too good for it."

"Me?" she chuckled. "I don't feel so pure. And we weren't married. We were together two months tops."

"Pure is a concept in someone's mind which isn't based on sex," Sean said, giving her a smile he hoped would help. "It can be tangible like being kind to a kid or petting his cat. Puts you in a class above most people."

"Really? You think like that?"

"Ah...huh," he mumbled. He kissed the back of her hand.

"With last night," Allonzo said," I would say he is mixing his insanities. These don't go together unless he was warped before he got here."

"His book collection was so damn creepy I wanted out."

"What books?"

"*Helter Skelter, Mind Hunters*. Biographies on Dalmer and the Zodiac and more. Lots more. His book case was full of them. I went out one day and stayed out. I went to a friend's house."

"Susan."

She nodded.

"What about your house?" Sean asked.

"My house is in the foothills of San Fernando Valley. It takes a long time to commute. I would've gone back in a few days, but I was trying to decompress. I have five roommates and I didn't want to face them."

"You have five roommates?" Sean asked.

She nodded. "Um…huh. Four in the house and one in the guest house."

"Do I pay you that badly?"

"Oh no," she said. "It's my mom. She's sick."

Sean sat forward to look at her.

"My sister lives with her in Bakersfield, but they think I'm this Hollywood big-shot with money to burn. Insurance covers the treatment, but there is nothing around for rent and food and other stuff. I send up every dime I can. So does my other sister, Marsha. She lives in The Bay area and does pretty well in banking."

"And you live frugally."

"I have to."

"Explains the car," he smiled as he leaned back. She drove a ten-year old Ford Focus that looked like it ran on prayer.

Allonzo looked at her. "What's wrong with your mom?"

"She has Stage III Hodgkin's."

"Shit," Sean said, squeezing her hand.

"And Miles?" Allonzo asked.

"I didn't tell him any of this. And us, we would be warm at best. We had fun sometimes but it wasn't earth shattering. I don't understand why he would do something like this."

"Because he's a sociopath who's probably afraid of his own shadow. He was most likely obsessed to epic proportions before you were together. Then he got what he wanted. You were there and then you weren't. But in his mind, you didn't walk, you were stolen."

He pointed at Sean. "By you."

"You think seeing me kiss her set this off?"

"He was already fixated. Seeing what he saw though, that did pull you into it and it explains to him why she left. She couldn't have gone on her own. In his mind, she had to be tempted away."

"She became the whore," Sean said. "One kiss and he trades her from Madonna to whore?"

"Probably."

"Why not—" Sean stopped, not looking at her directly. "I am sorry this is a horrible question. Last night. He had her there for hours with opportunity, but he didn't. Was this that Madonna thing?"

"Could be. He's probably pretty smart, too. Goes with the territory. He might have figured out that even with a condom he could leave DNA behind. Another man's DNA at a crime scene with you at the center?" Allonzo shook his head. "He might get caught."

Sean leaned back and closed his eyes. "That's just fucking twisted."

"You're a security guard," she said. "This doesn't sound like routine security guard territory."

"Okay," Allonzo smiled.

Sean glanced at her. "My family's been dealing with problems like these for two generations, Beth. I had my share before and it was pretty calm, but when Adian was born, I fired what I had and got better. Everyone under Allonzo is military trained with highly tuned skills. No one is getting near my son and no one is getting near you."

"You're scary?" she asked Allonzo.

"Never to you, pretty lady."

"Allonzo was the first I got even before Elaine moved out. It's why he gets away with so much shit."

Allonzo smiled and blew him a kiss.

"Foot massage?" Sean offered.

"No," Allonzo said. "But I would like you two to realize its two days before a holiday and this is the time when people relax. Which is why we will be going on overdrive with security on this place."

"What?" Beth asked. "I have to go home. My mom is in Bakersfield. They're expecting me."

"Are they expecting you looking like you just went four rounds with Mike Tyson?"

"Oh, damn," she mumbled, sinking into the cushions.

"What about you?"

"Mom was coming down to Charlie's place. Mark was talking about going over with the family."

"Can you get out of it?"

"Mom will give me hell at Christmas but yeah. I don't think it will be a problem. Not the first time a Branigan missed a holiday on account of show business."

Beth sat on the edge of the bed she now shared with Sean, Donnatello's fat ass next to her, and turned over, tummy up beside her. She dialed on Sean's phone as she scratched the cat's stomach. Angela picked up at once.

"Hey," Beth said.

"This isn't your phone. This came in as Unknown."

"Yeah, I figured it would. My phone kinda got lost so I had to borrow one."

"What's up? You sound like shit."

"How's mom?"

"Her treatment was Tuesday. She's been pretty weak. Can't really eat yet, but she's better. Why didn't you call? You usually call."

"Um," was as far as she made it.

"Beth, what's going on?"

"I'm sorry. There was a problem here."

"At work?"

"No, this was more personal and it kind of got nasty. I'm not seeing Miles anymore and I've started staying with a friend."

54

"My God, what happened?"

"Miles turned out to be more than the icky feeling I told you about."

"Are you okay?"

"Will be. I have some friends helping me out. I can't tell you more about it. I know them from work."

"TV people?"

"Yeah, you could say they're TV people. I'm not going to get home on Thursday."

"What? You can't miss Thanksgiving. Mom needs you here and you know it could be—"

"Angela, I got hurt bad. It all shows and I can promise you, seeing me won't help mom. It will make it worse."

"Are you alright? What happened?"

"After I broke up with Miles, I went back to pick some stuff. He was waiting."

"Did he hurt you?"

"Yes."

"Did he...?"

"No. A friend intervened. I'm staying at his place in his mom's room. His son is here, too."

"What's his name?"

She hesitated. "His name is Sean. That's all I'll tell you."

Angela laughed a little. "Really? Then tell me this. How many Sean's work on the set of *Snap Shots*."

Beth let out a breath. "Damn."

"Is he really as cute in person?"

"I could've told you that five years ago. What's really going through that nasty mind of yours is—does he kiss as good as it looks on screen."

"And?"

Beth smiled. "Better."

"You're not staying in his mom's room."

"I am," Beth said. "And I'm not. But there is nothing going on. Please don't tell mom. Tell Marsha, but don't tell mom, okay?"

"But you're okay, right? Nothing broken, nothing missing?"

"Just banged up."

"I think you're probably in good hands though I wish I knew more."

"Tell mom the set burned down and we're rebuilding it or something."

Sean came in, sitting down beside her. He leaned over to nuzzle her neck and she squirmed until his arm held her still.

"I gotta go, Angela. I'm sorry about the holiday. I'll make it up at Christmas."

She disconnected the call, and he reached up to cup her jaw, pulling her toward him for a wildly hot kiss of decadence that should not exist in circumstances that felt unreal. But he tasted good and his hands on her body felt better. When he made that little noise, she probably would agree to any plan he came up with.

He put his forehead on hers, and closed his eyes.

"I am sorry," he said, "if I made you feel more scared or unsure this morning. I didn't mean to. I was processing it and everything I wanted to do and say was getting jumbled."

She looked up at him. "Thank you. For that and everything else."

"Thank you for staying. I really would prefer you did it on your own rather than me having to lock you up someplace."

She smiled and winced. "Please don't make me laugh."

He touched her face gently with the pads of his fingers. "You did a good job," he said. "I can barely tell. Even the swelling looks less and I know it's still there."

"You still want to kiss me like this? All made up to hide the ugly?"

Holding the tip of her chin in his fingers, he brushed his lips on hers lightly.

He whispered, very softly. "I plan on kissing these lips when they are old, grey, withered, dried out and turned to leather. So yeah. I think I can handle a few days of Hollywood magic."

CHAPTER FIVE

Thursday was another sleep in day. When the doorbell rang, Sean slipped away quietly to take care of whoever was here on Thanksgiving morning before getting back to bed. Until noon pulled them all up, then it was time to phone all their mothers: Sean, Beth and Adian.

"Mom, stop," Sean said. "It can't be helped, I can't change it and this is the way it is. You can guilt me about it till Christmas."

Beth's went better, though he saw it pained her to say the words. "I can't get up there, Mom. I tried. No, it' not work." She looked at Sean. "It's the car, Mom. I think it might finally be dying. There is no way it will make up Tejon Pass." She closed her eyes, her fingers rubbing her forehead. "I know. I know."

She hung up looking close to tears.

"I'm sorry, Beth," he said.

"I hate lying to her."

It took three tries to get Adian to go near the phone to call Elaine.

"Five minutes," Sean promised. "You know she won't go past that."

"But I hate it." Adian's whine leaned more toward age four than thirteen.

He dialed the number he didn't have programed into favorites.

She was with her new boyfriend for the holiday. Which was strange as it had been her year to have Thanksgiving with Adian. She apologized again for being out of the country.

"I know you understand," Sean heard her say on the speakerphone.

Why hadn't he wrung her neck in her sleep, he didn't know.

Adian hung up and looked at the display. "Six minutes, twelve seconds. I'm taking that extra minute off the next one."

"Come on," Sean said, taking her by the hand and leading her to the media room.

He sat her down in front of the big screen. The couch was a wrap around, the size of the TV obscene, but the window had heavy covering to block out the low cast day.

Adian sat a Coke and a bowl of popcorn beside her.

Sean leaned over from behind the couch and slapped the remote into her hand then kissed her on the cheek.

"You stream whatever you want while we get everything ready."

"I usually do dress up on Thanksgiving. And we always eat by three."

He looked at his watch. "Missed that and those are damn cute pajamas. You have your borrowed face on and it's time to relax and let us get this."

She looked up at him.

"I put extra butter on the popcorn," Adian said. "It's a holiday."

She smiled. An orange and white cat jumped on her and flopped over to press on her leg.

The men disappeared into the kitchen, leaving her alone for the first time. Sean was aware and made sure he could hear her if she needed anything.

The Thanksgiving dinner, that was delivered this morning, was on the counter, having come to room temperature. Nothing was spared and there was enough food to feed an army. Turkey, stuffing, cranberry sauce and yams. He made sure there were two pies for choices and a pumpkin mousse. They would be eating from the leftovers for three days minimum.

Going to the garage, he brought in the elaborate bouquet of flowers Allonzo brought last night. Oranges, yellows and purples. It screamed fall and smelled wonderful as he put it on the table.

Adian finished setting the table with the good dishes Sean's mom made him buy. Now, Sean stood back to look at their work and thought maybe mom wasn't wrong all the time, not that he would tell her, he smiled.

A family Thanksgiving. He had sat at tables with everyone he cared about and it didn't come close to how, right this minute, this Thanksgiving felt. They were a family stepping into their first holiday together.

"Dad?"

"Humph," Sean said, moving the vase two inches to the right.

"Do you hear that?" Adian chuckled.

Absorbed in his thoughts, Sean had to admit he hadn't been paying as close attention as he should have.

The TV was on in the other room, the volume set a little high.

"You're fucking kidding me," he laughed.

He went through the house to where she sat. On the screen in front of her, five feet high, was *him*.

"This is what you went with?"

She looked up at him and smiled. "You said I could watch what I want."

"I thought you might go with *Lord of the Rings* or something. Didn't actually think you would download *me*."

"I've seen *Lord of the Rings*."

"You've seen *Days Gone Bad* four times. You told me."

She patted the seat next to her.

"You want me to watch *my* movie with you?"

She pointed to the spot next to her on the other side, beside the cat. "Adian here."

The men looked at each other.

"Hey," Sean said to Adian. "You're the one who wants to keep her."

Adian laughed and hopped over to the couch, landing in his position. He grabbed the popcorn and put it in his lap.

Sean walked around, moved the cat over and sank into the spot next to her. He picked up her hand and she leaned on him, her head on his shoulder.

She pointed at the screen. "Okay," she said, "right here. Wait for it."

He didn't really have a clue what he had said on the screen. He was never overly comfortable watching a performance after the release, but right now, it seemed fine.

"Okay," she said, looking up at him. "That was brilliant. And you don't even realize how wonderful it is until you see the movie twice because you don't know this whole scene is a set up. You come back and it's 'oh my God how did I miss that?' This is good," she smiled. "This is really good."

He leaned over and kissed her on the cheek.

She talked pretty much the whole time and neither Sean nor Adian complained. Adian got them all drinks and made sure the food wasn't going bad while Sean saw his work through someone else's eyes, someone he truly cared about. Her opinion mattered.

When the final credits went by, he was watching her.

"Adian?"

"Yeah."

"You think the four boys could stand one more kitten?"

Adian laughed. "You want another cat?"

"No, Beth does."

She was looking up at him. There were three cats in various positions within ten feet of them.

"She's had the name picked out for a while."

"It will probably throw us off a little, but get a girl cat and I bet she whips these guys into shape."

"Why don't you go get everything on the table?"

Adian winked at him with a smirk and went back the same way he came.

Sean grabbed her around the shoulder, pulled her tight and laid them back on the couch, her under him. His kiss was deep and thorough with more purpose than even he expected.

Her arms were around him, rubbing his back. She kissed him back, her tongue on his making him nuts.

He pulled back a little, keeping her close.

"I want you to marry me," he said looking in her eyes.

She choked out a laugh that was more gasp. "The commentary was that good?"

"Long term," he said, kissing her again. "I told you I want long term."

"That's...um…a nice offer. But…"

"What? But what?"

"It's only been a couple of days."

"Bullshit. Maybe officially it's only been a couple. The courtship has been going for months. I want this."

"No?" she said with no conviction.

"Okay," he smiled and kissed her harder, deeper. He sucked her resolve right out of her. His hand covered her breast, loving the feel of something he didn't get very often: natural. Soft and yielding. She arched her back, pushing into him until he made her moan.

Too turned on for his own good, he pulled back and slid his hand down to her hip.

"If I made my point," he whispered, kissing her neck. "I think dinner is ready."

"I think you might be a bastard," she said but she smiled when she said it.

"I think you are right and I will change your mind."

"Does anyone ever say no to you?"

"All the time. I'm just not accepting it this time."

"Um…dinner is ready," Adian said from the door. "I even opened the wine."

"She said no," Sean said as he helped her sit.

Adian came to the couch. "What? What did you do wrong?"

Her gaze snapped to Adian and Sean laughed.

"It's a conspiracy, you understand. And you don't stand a chance in hell of walking away. If I don't convince you, he's going to do his puppy face and you will be toast."

The day after Thanksgiving, they were still holed up at the house. Two security guards patrolled on the outside, Allonzo called a couple of times a day. The restraining order was in place.

Adian took the pumpkin mousse out to the guards.

"What was it like?" she asked, sipping at the wine. "Growing up like that? In that lifestyle?"

Sean and Beth sat in the grand living room among the works of art on the walls, the lit fireplace and sofas where a person could sink and get lost. The atmosphere was low light, the wine just right. The company in the chair across from her, too perfect for words. The cat in his lap—big, fat and grey. Sean scratched him absent-mindedly.

"Flash, I guess. A lot of show. Beverly Hills High was full of kids of stars or stars themselves. We were used to it. We were on the top rung of popularity because of who our parents were. I didn't like it even when I exploited it. It was great for getting dates."

"Do you think there was more pressure?"

"I don't know if it would be the right expression," he said. He took a sip of his red wine. "My parents did the best they could, but their careers came first. We always knew that and accepted it. Until the divorce, they tried to make sure one of them was always home but then one took a play in New York for six months while the other had a movie they were making. A lot of holidays got missed. A lot of important events in school."

"But you had money."

"I still do. Don't think it's actually the way to be happy. Nice cars and house are okay, but a night like this is even better and we could do this in a cabin. What about you?"

She laughed and drank a little more.

"Bakersfield, capitol of the dullest childhood history. We had our football games on Fridays. We had Thrifty Drugs because there was no Walmart. We got our ice creams there and cheap make-up three sisters shared. Boys thought they were entitled because there was nothing else to do and girls stayed after school to work on projects with some teacher just for the experience. Most kids drank a lot on the weekend. Pot was popular with some. The ones who couldn't take the life, went further with drugs or escaped to LA."

"Were you a cheerleader?"

"No," she smiled. "Never went that route though I bet we could get a uniform in my size."

He looked at her and smiled wide. "I think you are trying to tempt me."

"I think one of us has to do the tempting before you get tired of me."

He watched her for a long minute, with a slight smile. "I'm not going to get tired of you, Beth. That I know."

Adian came in hiding something behind his back.

"I'm bored."

"Go clean something," his dad said.

"Not that kind of bored."

"That's the only bored there is."

Adian pulled a box from behind him and held it for the two of them to see.

"You're kidding," she laughed.

"What's wrong with Twister?" Adian asked.

He dropped to the carpet and pulled out the pieces. He arranged the sheet, smoothing it flat and then grabbed the spinner. Then he smiled up at her.

"You're serious?" she asked.

Rotten kid could smile just like his dad.

Sean put his glass on the table, tossed the cat to the floor and leaned forward laughing.

"You're first," he said to her.

Adian's finger was ready to snap the spinner.

Officially, it was the Christmas season.

Adian went to school driven by Kevin, one of Allonzo's men, every morning as usual. Kevin picked him up, too. Sean took the Audi to the studio and made Hollywood look good. He was only working half days, but it was still a long time.

Beth stayed at the house while her face healed, sleeping in his bed and she began to want more in the nights than the cuddles.

She was alone with the cats most of the time, but they were good company. They took to her like she belonged there. At least one fur ball was always within arm's length. Tummy's were rubbed.

Sean hadn't mentioned it again.

The marriage thing.

But she got the feeling he was letting her come to her own conclusion.

Which he was positive would be his conclusion.

Finding his American Express Gold Card on the counter one morning, she used her new phone to call him at the office.

"What's up?"

"You left your Gold Card here. I didn't want you to think you lost it."

"That's for you."

"What?" she managed.

"I figured you might be bored and Christmas is coming up. I thought you could buy me something amazing and barely there."

She chuckled. "You want *me* to use *your* credit card to buy *stuff for you?*"

"Honey, buy whatever you want. It's good with no strings. I have to go, though. They're staring at me."

"Who's staring at you?"

"People who think they wield more power than I do."

"Yeah, they've never tried to get you to be reasonable. You're sure of this?"

"Bye," he laughed.

She made a pot of tea in the plain white pot they had and glanced every now and then at the card.

No, she thought. It wouldn't be right. She smiled anyway.

The clothes on her back right now, plus those in the closet and drawers, were ordered for her by him without her knowledge, saving them all a trip to the Foothills to get her own. He had good taste, she thought. And he bought the right size and not the sizes he was used to.

Taking her tea in both hands, she walked through to the living room, wondering in which corner they put their tree. She wondered what two guys living together really knew about Christmas decorations. So far, nothing had even been mentioned.

She went to her laptop, brought up an online store and found a cute Santa Claus teapot. This one might be more fun than their white one. When she added it to her cart, she was told that this item was usually purchased with a matching mug and tray. She smiled and added them, too, going back for the cookie jar and candle holder.

Without hesitation she went to the kitchen for the card.

Two days later when they arrived and were out, neither of the men did more than smile.

The red tablecloth came next but it was the centerpiece on the kitchen table that made her feel like Christmas in this house was around the corner: a large glass vase, filled with red, white and gold bulbs. It was full of water and had three candles floating and lit. She put a smaller, matching one by the front door.

She put more decorations out and saw them look it over or pick something up to look at it closely, but neither said anything.

She made dinners and baked Christmas sugar cookies.

They ate them all.

"About that question," he tried as he wrapped his arm around her from behind to kiss her neck. She was putting the final changes on the fancy dinner of hot dogs and beans.

"No."

She felt him smile against her neck.

"K," he said moving to the fridge to get a beer.

The bedding in both their bedrooms was next.

Washed in Downy.

She probably went too young with Adian's with the bright red giant Santa Clause, a sack over his shoulder. But he didn't complain. She heard the squeal and the laugh then saw his smile.

For Sean, she went more mature. Mostly red and white with stripes. When made up with all the accessories, it looked like a giant present.

"I am not having sex in a Christmas present."

"You're not having sex now," she pointed out.

He glared at her then moved into the closet to change.

It felt like home and for the two weeks it took her face to return to normal, she took their house and turned it into a holiday event. Gifts, decorations, candles burning in bayberry. The only thing missing was the tree.

"We get the tree the week before," he told her. "About twenty feet tall and yes, we decorate it all ourselves. Try to get some rest," he smiled. "I don't want to tire you out."

CHAPTER SIX

Walking down the hall to the door as she had for five years, she smiled and greeted her co-workers and no one asked questions or made comments.

She reached the door with her name on it—always happy to have her own little space—and stepped inside, flipping on the switch to light the place up.

She froze as the door closed behind her. Too shocked to do anything else while minutes ticked by. Her gaze traveled the room until her feet began to move.

She went to her desk, put her purse and books down on the available space, then pulled out her phone to scroll to Allonzo.

It was picked up on the first ring.

"Hi," she said. "This is Beth Hardwick."

"Hey pretty lady. What can I do for you?"

"Allonzo?"

"That's right."

"Could you send someone to my office? Quick."

His tone changed. "Is there a problem?"

"Maybe," she said, hearing her voice hitch. "Could you hurry? I don't think I want to be alone."

"I'm on my way."

Sean sat at his seat, a yellow pad in front of him, his scribbled notes taking up space. The last script before Christmas break was open beside the pad and his handwriting decorated it. Around the table, seven people were taking their own notes on words he had written.

The spindly tree in the corner could have been done with more imagination, he thought, his concentration breaking at the never-ending drone of this two-hour meeting. He looked at the tree and thought, what with this being Hollywood, weren't they supposed to be creative and shit?

He barely noticed when executive assistant, Janine, walked in. She wasn't his executive assistant. Until it was him she walked up to, leaning over to whisper in his ear.

"You have a phone call."

He glanced up. "Did you tell them I was in a meeting?"

"He didn't seem to care. Said you would want to take this."

"Who?"

"He was with security."

Sean's gaze snapped up and the cold settled over him.

He put his hands on the table and pushed off. "Excuse me," he said to the impatient people.

He took the call at the phone in the corner.

"What?"

"I thought I should let you know. I'm heading out to your little lady's office and we're on STAT."

"Why? What happened?"

"I don't know. She didn't tell me. But she was scared to death and she said she didn't want to be alone. I thought you would want to know."

The phone disconnected and he hung up, not liking any of the words or the order they were delivered in. He cleared his throat, went back to his seat, pulled his coat off the back and looked at the perturbed faces.

"Bye," he said, turning toward the door and leaving everything he had brought with him behind.

"You can't leave," Ted laughed. "It's the last script before Christmas. We need your notes."

He turned as he walked backwards. "It's my script, Ted. It is my notes."

"You can't do this," Carol added.

"Yes I can. I'm the boss. I can do whatever I want," he smiled.

He hit the door with his back. Then he took the stairs, jumping into slow jog that took him the distance between the offices and the prop department. Allonzo was going in.

"Wait," Sean said, a little hot, a little sweaty.

They found her together and she jumped out of her skin when they opened the door. She was seated in her chair, pushed back away from her desk, hands in her lap.

The entire room was destroyed. Books slashed on the shelves and floor, the desk broken in a corner. Posters of projects she had worked on were ripped off the wall. Not one single item was spared. The room smelled of smoke and Allonzo went looking for the cause while Sean went around the desk, kneeling in front of her and picked her hands in his. She was shaking, her face pale, her breathing hard.

"He didn't like me," she said, looking down. "Not really. There was barely anything there. This doesn't make sense."

Sean sighed, reached up and ran his hand over her hair.

He glanced at Allonzo. Allonzo was on the other side of the desk, holding a metal trash can. He looked up and Sean followed his gaze. The smoke detector was ripped off.

Allonzo pulled out a charred scrap. "It's your script. I bet all these are your scripts."

"How the hell did he get in here?"

"Office was empty for a while. There's no actual smoke, just the smell. That can linger for weeks."

Sean stood up. "But he got in. He was fired. He shouldn't be able to get back on the lot." He looked down at her.

"Branigan, we don't even know which one of you he is after. Burning your scripts is a pretty good indication and if he knows about you two, hurting her would hurt you. Makes her a target regardless."

"Okay, fine. She's a target with a bodyguard 24/7."

"Puts one of us at the house all the time."

"I don't give a fuck. Are we clear? Get someone over here. And call the police."

"We could handle this inside."

"We could but getting another report might help later."

"Are you asleep," he whispered softly, so not to wake her if she wasn't.

She didn't move, didn't turn toward him. "I think today was a little too surreal to doze."

"I would kill to sleep with you. You have to know that even if I don't."

She laughed a little. "I find it hard to believe."

He waited, debating reaching out to touch her. "I've dated a lot of women."

"The entire world knows you've dated a lot of women."

"I slept with all of them."

"Shocker," she said to him.

"Roll over so I can see you."

She waited, but did start to move. It was slow though, as if it hurt. He put his hand on her arm rubbing, trying to bring comfort. She slowly settled into the pillow, her eyes closed.

She opened her eyes and blinked.

"I don't want to do that with you. I want us to do it different which is why I asked."

"I'm usually up for different with only minor restrictions provided there's a safe word."

"You're not going to let me say this, are you?"

"I am hoping to avoid it, yes."

"I want different. I want something innocent that lasts."

"Can't you do that now? I mean maybe not me, but you have to have a phone number which works."

"I don't want that. I want you to stay here."

"We've been having a lot of fun. I know that. Playing house with you and Adian is beyond wonderful, but you have to know it's not going to last."

"I spent most my life chasing things I didn't want then saw the one I had been looking for all along and she was on someone else's arm."

"Can I ask you a question that's none of my business?"

"Sure. I will answer anything you want."

She licked her lips and waited. "I am out of line here but I'm curious. I'm pretty damn sure you have sole custody and it's rare for a dad to get that, especially with who his mom is."

"I do," he said. "He's all mine."

He stared at her, bracing his hand under his head. "Elaine is a piece of work," he said. "I'm talking off the charts nut job. I don't care how gorgeous she is or what kind of a career she had. She had these rules that she followed. Some were based on another planet. We were only together for two months when I wanted out. I couldn't take her anymore. But I found out she was pregnant. The way I found out—the abortion clinic called me to verify the appointment. She had put me down as partner, didn't tell me and they called me instead of her."

"She didn't want him?"

"She didn't want him then, she doesn't want him now. Not really. I agreed to full custody right away. It's how I stopped that appointment."

He broke off and rolled onto his back.

"What?"

He turned his face toward her. "He doesn't know this. I've never told him. Don't know if I would."

"You don't have to tell me."

He rolled back over. "Do you know what she wanted in exchange to stop the abortion? She wanted me to pay for an extended shopping spree to Paris. And she wanted a Picasso. I had to find a fucking Picasso that she liked and she *hates* Picasso.

Her net worth is twice mine and she is a lunatic. Great in bed, but oh, so not worth it."

She reached up to rub his hair, scooting a little closer.

"I'm sorry," she said.

"She burned it," he said. "She said it reminded her of me, so she burned it and then took off for France on my dime and I had to wait three agonizing months to find out if she had gotten a doctor over there to do it."

"She makes pretty babies," she said quietly.

It took him a second to laugh and look toward her.

"But she had help," she continued. "And the good manners, and good discussions and just all around great kid, I think that was all his dad's doing."

He was smiling when he grabbed her around the waist and pulled her close. He buried his face in her neck. "Say yes."

"No."

He sighed. "Why not?"

"I have to know its real first and I can't know that right now, not like this."

"This feels pretty damn real."

"It's not what I meant and you know it."

He sighed again, loosened his hold a bit and let them both settle onto the same pillow.

"We tried the family routine when he was born, living at my house. I wanted to do it for him. It was a nightmare. He would cry and she wouldn't touch him, wouldn't feed him. She didn't want anything to do with him. She said 'it wasn't normal for them to be like that.'"

"Them?"

"Babies. I cancelled the engagement, took three years off, wrote two books and hired a nanny when he was ready."

She stared at him, a small smile on her lips. "You did good," she smiled.

"Thank you."

"He is really a good kid."

Sean smiled. "I think so, too. He can be a pretty big pain in the ass, but you get used to it. You know, I've never told anybody any of this."

"Why not?"

"Not their business. They didn't ask. They didn't care. I never wanted it out, especially about the misplaced phone call. I don't want her name to get out with that kind of information. It might hurt him."

"You told me."

"Yes, I did. Funny how that works."

She was quiet for a long minute.

"I have a problem, Sean," she said, scared. "It's been weeks and he's still out there."

"*We* have a problem. This is you and me, with Adian's help. All of us taking care of us."

She blinked and tilted her chin.

"That's kind of a huge commitment with someone who said no."

Leaning over he kissed her softly. "So far. I'm not done yet."

With new scripts on a folding table in a room not hers, Beth went through the motion of reading and tried not to think about what happened in this very building. They were doing normal, they were doing every day. He was at work. She was at work. Adian was at school.

The fact Jared sat in another chair reading a *Sports Illustrated* while on alert, made her feel a little better. He *was* on alert, she knew that even as he looked down and seemed bored. Every one of Allonzo's men would kill or die to keep her safe.

She sat the purple highlighter down and closed the script. She leaned back in her chair, sighed harder than intended.

Mr. 'On Alert' put the magazine down and looked at her. "Everything okay?"

He was cute, she thought. Blond hair with brown eyes. Not the kind she would look at twice, but not bad on a billboard.

She closed her eyes and couldn't believe she thought that.

"I can't do this," she said.

"Can't do what, ma'am?"

"Sit here, in this building, pretending what happened didn't happen. It's like a hundred feet from here."

"I'm kind of curious. Can I ask what you do here?"

"I'm a script reader."

He shook his head with a tilted chin.

"I go over the scripts to figure out what props they will need for the show. Vases, guns, a puppy. Whatever."

He smiled. "That's pretty cool. I've never met a script reader."

"Just a scared to death female with a lunatic out there after her?"

He nodded and smiled like it was no big deal. "Those, I've met."

"Cute," she smiled.

"The room is there. He's not. There is nothing to worry here. You can work."

"I can't concentrate."

"Where do you want to go?"

"My car. I can put this away and then grab Sean."

"Okay," he smiled. He wore a black T-shirt, a jacket over it to hide the gun he had on under his arm.

She actually hated guns.

She put everything into her brown leather messenger bag, then hooked it over her shoulder. She knew he would never offer to carry the load. His hands had to be free. He wasn't here to valet. He was here to protect.

They walked together to the parking lot. Christmas hadn't reached this area of the lot. Too much going on for production. And then, break at the end of the week, so no one would care.

She came around the corner to her parking spot and stopped, staring at her Ford Focus.

She caught a movement out of the corner of her eye, and looked up to see Miles on the other side of the fence in the brush. He drew a finger across his throat, before darting into the mountain of bushes which surrounded the studio.

"Did you see that?" she whispered, hoarse.

"See what?" Jared asked. His gun drawn and he was making a circle.

"Over there," she pointed. "He was over there."

Jared didn't move. He wasn't leaving her side. He grabbed his radio and got Allonzo on the horn.

She stepped back, and started to shake. She couldn't look at the car. She had to get away.

Turning, she headed toward the offices.

"Ms. Hardwick," Jared yelled. "You have to stay here. You can't be alone."

She kept going and he caught up to her. She heard him tell Allonzo they had left the scene with no destination.

She reached Sean's building, went up the stairs instead of the elevator and got to his floor.

She walked past the receptionist, ignoring the protests to stop. She did stop, on this side of the door.

She turned to Jared. "Can you wait out here, please?"

He sighed. "Leave the door open. I am right here and you are safe."

She nodded.

Her heart pounding, her breath caught in her chest, she kept her gaze down.

Sean was standing by the window and he turned as the door opened, his voice mingling with that of whoever was on the speakerphone.

She looked up and saw mild shock on his face.

"Martin," he said to the air. "I'll call you back." He disconnected the call before Martin agreed or had a chance to reply.

But she didn't know what to say.

"What?" he finally asked. "Where's Jared?"

She pointed toward the door, swallowing. "Miles was downstairs."

"Miles can't get on the lot. We made sure of it."

"Miles was downstairs," she repeated. "I saw him. Jared didn't."

"Did he say anything?"

She looked at him, tears on her face "He—" She looked down and drew her finger across her neck. Then she peered up at him.

He hit the speaker button again, dialing a number, the beeps so damn loud.

The deep voice answered.

"Allonzo?"

"We're at the car now. And Michael and Seth just went in the direction she said. Is she with you?"

"Yeah. Too shaken. What the hell happened?"

"I'll check in when I know more. You want police here?"

"Yeah. More reports." He disconnected the call.

"It was only a couple of seconds," she said. "But he stared at me," she said, wrapping her arms around herself.

He came around the desk toward her. "What about the car?"

"It had blood on it. Words, I think. I think they were for me."

He rubbed his hands up and down her arms. "What did they say?"

She looked at him, feeling the tears run down her cheek.

"You're gonna die bitch."

"Fuck," he mumbled, pulling her close. "Jared?" He shouted.

The security man came in.

"Nothing?"

"I saw the car. She said she saw him take off. I stayed with her and called in the info. I don't have any more yet."

"What do I do? I don't know what to do."

"Jared, can you wait outside?"

The man left and closed the door.

"First off," he said quietly, "you're fired."

She took a step back, staring at him. "What?"

"You're going to either stay at the house or be in this building."

"You can't take away my job. I need it. My mom."

"Alright. Leave of absence then. With pay. On a time I determine until this is over."

"You can't do this," she said. "I need my job. I can't afford not to have it."

"You don't need it anymore and you know it."

"I haven't agreed to anything with you."

"You're living with me, Beth. Do you understand that? You just charged up my AmEx to its limit and AmEx doesn't even have a limit."

She stopped and took a breath. "It wasn't that much. It was a couple of things."

"We're living in the fucking North Pole and I seriously have no problem with that or the charges. I gave you the card to use.

But you have to realize what is going on here. This isn't playing house. Adian doesn't think you are my next date."

She took a step away from him.

He followed, grabbing her hands to pull her closer.

"All of this is a prelude to the next step which includes getting this asshole out of our lives so you stop looking like Bambi gone wild."

"This isn't your problem, Sean. It never was."

He took a step forward, reaching up to hold her. "We're going to forget the fact that it was *me* he lured to that condo. Let's focus on the reality. Why did you come here?"

"What do you mean?"

"You could have stayed down there, called the police yourself. Jared is right there. He would have taken care of everything. Why come to me? If it's not my problem, why drag me in?"

She took a step back. "I never wanted to drag you into anything. He took the phone and—"

"I would've found out later what he did to you. I didn't have to drop everything I was doing and go but I did. And even he knew I would. You think I would've wanted to find out about you hurt through the grapevine?"

She covered her face in her hands and then softly pulled them down.

"This is *our* problem, honey. You say yes or no, it doesn't matter. We're seeing this through together."

CHAPTER SEVEN

Four more days of house arrest and there were no more Christmas things to buy. She had the radio programmed to continuous playing of Christmas music to try to change the tone of the house and neither of her men seemed to mind.

With warm eggnog by her computer, she sat at the table going over the notes she had typed up for a story which came to mind.

There was no danger in it.

No stalkers.

No cops.

It was one she could really get into.

Sean finished loading the dishwasher and came to lean on the table. He was working from home now. Christmas break was in a few days, so he could play more. He didn't have to be back at the studio for weeks.

"What are you working on?"

"Story notes," she said, without looking up.

"Am I in them?"

"Yeah, you're the homeless guy on the corner with the sign that says 'Needs Miracle.'"

He leaned over and kissed her neck. "I already have mine."

She smiled. She loved it when he said stuff like that.

"I'm going to go take a shower. Back in twenty."

"Sure." She looked up at him. "Did you want something for dinner?"

He bobbed his head. "We'll figure something out."

She drank her eggnog feeling the holiday cheer. It was easy to do that here, to forget. It was Christmassy and the music comforted like a warm blanket. She could get used to this and she was afraid he was right. She was going to cave. Which actually wasn't scary at all.

She opened her e-mail and scanned the list of incoming, started to open a 'compose' when something set her off, things weren't quite right.

It took a second for her to focus on the problem.

Every single little box under incoming was marked 'read'. Even in the letters she had yet to open and read. Her mom's, her sister's, a letter of confirmation on a book order. Two for work and an advertisement.

All marked 'read'.

Except for the one at the top. The one that just came in.

The sender was 'alternativetolegal@gmail.com

She had no idea who it was or what it meant.

She hit open and the file downloaded, taking longer than usual due to the photo coming in.

When it blinked done then flashed, she sucked in a breath and fell against the chair.

Instantly her hand shot up, slamming her laptop shut. She looked around to make sure no one saw it. She could hear Adian playing his game upstairs. Sean was still in the shower.

What to do first thoughts ran through her head in rapid succession.

She grabbed the machine, tucked it under her arm and walked into the steamy bathroom, closing the door hard and sitting the computer on the damp counter.

He opened the glass door and she averted her eyes as she lifted the lid of the laptop and pulled up the photo.

"You do realize we're not sleeping together in the biblical sense so technically you aren't supposed to barge in and find me naked."

She turned the computer so he could see it.

He stared at it for several seconds, his expression going cold. He turned off the spray.

"It was in my mailbox from some weird address."

He grabbed the towel off the rod, did a spot dry then wrapped it around his hips before stepping out. His long hair still dripped.

"The marquee," she said. "Look at the date on the marquee."

"It's today's," he said, looking more unsure, more scared than she ever saw him.

The close up of a smiling Adian coming out of school was an engaging photo. But the bulls-eye drawn over his face changed the whole image. The words *'count down starts now'* was enough to chill the blood and the brain.

"All my emails were read. He got into my computer, Sean. He got into my life and he took this picture."

"There's no way to prove it anymore then we could prove the text."

"Sean, I have to go."

"Oh fuck you," he snapped. "You aren't getting two feet toward the door."

"I go, Miles goes and Adian's safe," she pointed at the screen.

"We don't know what his plan is or who he wants."

She shook her head. "No. He knows this would drive me away. He knows I would do it for Adian."

"Fine, we'll go with that theory. And it doesn't make a goddamn difference. He knows what you'll do then he's waiting and you still are not getting two feet toward the door."

"What about Elaine?" she asked.

Sean, staring at the picture, shook his head. "He won't go."

"He has to. This isn't a problem a call to Allonzo will fix."

He looked at her. "He can't stand her, Beth. I told you. She's bat shit crazy and tries to drag him into the whacked crap she's into. He only sees her when he does because the courts say he has to. I probably would get him out of it if I could, but she'll come after us and I wasn't kidding. She's better financed with better lawyers."

"She didn't seem to be a problem for you before."

"Fourteen years ago I didn't look as closely to the conversation as I should have. It was a mistake. She was a mistake, but he wasn't so I can't regret her."

"What do we do?"

He looked at her. "Besides acknowledge the fact you said we?" He laughed. "Call Allonzo."

Allonzo made much better time on his Ducati than the police did through the narrow Hollywood Hill streets. He brought Scott with him. Scott knew computers.

"Where's the laptop?"

Beth led him to the kitchen table where the offending letter awaited.

Scott pulled it up and stared for half a minute.

"On a personal level, this pisses me like hell. Professionally, we might have more trouble."

He began clicking away on the laptop while Sean stood to the side, his arms crossed. He glanced up at the den door upstairs. So far, Adian hadn't caught on. When the police reached here that will change.

"I was going to call you tonight," Allonzo said.

"About what?"

"I was keeping track of Criswell since the office. He left the radar. I had some friends help and we checked around to his condo and watering holes. He fucking left the planet."

"You do realize this is not actually a comforting thought?"

"Allonzo, if he's after me, won't me leaving here keep them safe?"

"Could," he said, with a tilt of his head. "I doubt it, though. He's done some bad shit in the past that someone didn't want anyone to know. The records were sealed."

"How did you get sealed records?" she asked.

His smiled broadened and he tilted his chin again. "Records are only as sealed as the people who seal them. Call the right person at the right place from a time in his life where he really messed up and some people like to talk."

"What did they say?" Sean asked.

Scott stopped typing and turned in the chair, looking up at Sean.

"Address is bogus and there's no trace on it. We're not going to find out who sent it."

"You don't think it was him?"

"Me, hell yeah," Allonzo said, "but it's also possible you picked up a harassment on your own. You have the career for it and probably burned enough people unknowingly. Hell, a fan can do this shit. And if it started at the same time as the attack on

Beth, we wouldn't be able to pull the two cases away from each other."

"I've actually had fans who went too far. This is *way* too far."

"But it could happen," Allonzo said. "I don't think it did. I think it's him but I'm telling you what any cop or lawyer is going to tell you. They'll not be able to separate the two because it could be the same."

"Same or not, that is a bulls-eye on my son's face."

"And we had blood on her car. Wasn't blood, by the way. It was the fake shit. Probably stolen from the prop department. He had a reputation in high school of anger issues and fights, was kicked out. There were two girls who said he went too far when they told him to stop."

"Miles is a rapist?" she asked.

"I think he's a lot more than that. Two went missing in his home town. Took years for the bodies to show up. Autopsies showed they were stabbed in the side with their throat slit."

"What," she said meekly, almost too quietly. "I stayed with him. I *slept* beside him."

"Police thought it was him but couldn't prove it. Then he came to LA and got honest work. If he was pulling runaways or something, there wouldn't be a record."

She sank into a seat, her ability to talk shut down. She stared at the table.

"With his reading material and four girls crying violence, two dead—"

"We get Adian pulled out of school. Today," Sean said. "Like now. He's not going back."

"I am on his signature card. I can take care of it while you deal with her." Allonzo nodded toward Beth. "I'll coordinate guards on the house and you two don't think of leaving without checking in with me."

Sean nodded.

"Scott," Allonzo said.

"Yeah?"

"I think your H.A.L.O. skills need work. Go spend the evening with the kid and let him beat your ass."

"He probably will anyway. I suck at H.A.L.O." He got up and followed the sounds of Adian's game.

"Beth," Sean said and she jumped at the sound of her own name.

Her gaze came up. "He made me breakfast a couple of times. You've made me breakfast."

"Two different situations honey," he said, coming around the table. He put a hand on her elbow. She rose like a zombie.

He moved her to the media room, grabbing a blanket from the couch. Helping her down to the couch, he picked up the remote and found *Long Odds*.

He hit play, tossed the remote down beside him and gathered her in his arms, the blanket over them.

She didn't look at the screen. She kept her head on his chest, her whole body shaking.

95

"Come on," he said, giving her a little shake. "I want to know what you thought of this one. It's supposed to be funny. Funny is good."

He hated watching himself but he would sit through a marathon if it brought her back.

It took twenty minutes into the story before she turned her head.

"Lekan was funnier than you."

"You think so? I thought I did okay."

"You did," she said. "I didn't say you were bad. I just said he was funnier."

The shaking was slowing down. "He's a stand-up comedian. I think that's the way it works."

"He only ended up with one girl and you got two and then they found and they weren't happy. You got to kiss both, though."

He hated watching these movies, but had to admit, he loved her commentaries.

She sat a little straighter. "See, this was a good character. It was real funny so you didn't have to do the deep drama which can be hard. When the viewer left this movie, they came away not worrying about anything. Everything was going to be—"

She broke off and sucked in a breath. The tears started before he even pulled her to him, he pressed her face to his chest with his hand on her head.

"What if he hurts him? Oh God, I can't live with that. He's just a bystander."

"We're better armed and if we're not, Allonzo has friends. He can bring them in."

"And you," she whispered. "I don't want you hurt over me."

"Same friends for all of us. We're going to take care of it. We're going to have Christmas and you're going to say yes and then all three of us are going away to some place."

"Where are we going?" she whispered. As she cried.

"I don't know. Where do you want to go?"

She turned her head so it was flat on his chest, his arms around her tight.

"Some place far away."

CHAPTER EIGHT

With eyes closed, she wrestled with her thoughts long after he fell asleep. The room dark, the shadows from the moon coming in the window, it was hard to know exactly what to do.

In the couple of days since the photo arrived, they hadn't left the house, none of them. And the heightened security around them looked normal now. They were getting used to it.

Sean made perfectly clear what he wanted.

Pulling the crush she had of the man in the movies away from the man who cared for her, had an edge of difficulty with it. She didn't want to disrespect him by being one of those followers. They had a relationship now. Adian, too. Inquisitive and sincere, always asking questions about what she was doing and her work.

Both of them. She had to grab this chance where she got the best of both and it felt real, like it would last.

He was face down when she rolled over. Naked to the waist with sweats on, the sheet and quilt rode low exposing his back.

His breathing was deep and rhythmic.

Very gently she ran a hand over his back, her palm flat, feeling the heat. He stirred. Stretching a little and settling further into the pillow.

Laying out beside him, she had to angle a little to meet his mouth. Kissing softly, she knew he was aware even in his sleep when he moved with her, toward her.

As he became awake, his hand traveled up her side, circling around to her back, pulling her closer. His mouth moved, opened, the taste and texture she came to know as his.

He didn't stop and she didn't try to dissuade. Not when he rolled away from her onto his back, pulling her with him. The kisses got hotter and deeper and she lay across his naked chest.

He was still holding her head, his fingers in her hair. She pulled back and straddled his middle, staring down at the beautiful face, alive right now with desire.

She brushed his hair behind an ear and then traced his lips with her finger.

"I'm thinking yes," she said, softly in the dark.

His breathing hard, he seemed like he was trying to focus. "No," he said. "I said I wouldn't. Not till later."

"I wasn't talking about that," she smiled, shy, looking down.

He shifted his head on the pillow, thinking long about what she was saying. "I'll hold you to it. There will never be a way out."

"I didn't think I would be looking for one."

He came off the mattress, a hand on either side of her face, bunching her hair in his fingers, then flipping them over to push her into the bed as his whole body covered hers, the kiss so hot, so deep it would suffocate if it wasn't so perfect.

"I will take you to bed on our wedding night, but not before."

"I still won't be thin enough, tall enough or have big enough boobs."

"Yeah, but you're not a bimbo either."

He kissed her softly. "Elaine will never let you adopt him, but she doesn't have a say in him calling you mom."

"Does he want to?"

Sean nodded.

"Mom," she whispered, feeling the word.

"This only started, you know, because I love you and have for a while. Just took a little bit of time to mesh it together."

She blinked at him, feeling the words and trying to understand them. They were too beautiful.

"I don't know about the timing, but I'm pretty sure I caught up with you."

He was smiling. "Can you say it?"

She wet her lips and bit the bottom one while he watched and waited.

She leaned forward, still across his body, until her mouth was beside his ear.

"I love you Sean Connor Branigan," she whispered, her voice so soft she barely heard it herself. She pulled back to look at him.

His eyes were closed, his grin huge.

With his arm still around her, she settled down, her head on his shoulder, her body running the length of his.

"I've never told a woman that," he said in the dark. "Never felt it with anyone else."

"So I can be the first?"

"And the last," he said.

Closing her eyes, she finally fell asleep.

He worked at his desk, his fingers' flying over the keyboard oblivious to the view of LA and oblivious to her curled up in the overstuffed chair next to the unlit fireplace. She balanced her notes on her lap, filling out the workbook on plotting the next story.

She had six written books to his two, two of hers available in print. When she got around to it, she would try to get the four out too, but so far, she was satisfied with having finished the stories.

She was trying to figure out her heroine's family background with her mechanical pencil when he leaned back in his chair, sighed hard and put his hands on his head. He didn't turn around toward her.

"What?" she asked.

"I'm trying to figure out why two relatively bright people would knowingly walk into a bar they knew was infested with supernatural bad guys."

She thought. "Amulets?"

"Season two," he said, still staring at his screen.

More silence. "Tattoos."

"Another show did it years ago."

"Okay," she sighed, thinking harder. She spoke slow. "Giant. Super. Soaker. Filled with holy water?"

He laughed and still didn't turn around. "Yeah. Um...I hadn't thought of that one. I'll give it a try."

When his fingers hit the keyboard, he was still chuckling and she smiled, watching him.

She went back to the chart in her workbook.

Do you ever want kids? it asked

"Sean?"

"Humph," he mumbled as he continued to type.

"Do you want more kids?"

He didn't pause as he kept on working. A good half a minute passed.

"I didn't actually plan on having the one I did. But it worked. Brat's not so bad."

She smiled again.

And he typed. She waited.

"Never really met anyone I would've wanted to take that route with, not even his mother."

Type. Silence. And she watched his back. When it seemed as if he was done, she looked at her workbook.

"Until I met you."

She smiled at the energy that surged through her gut.

"I wanted a big family," he said, still working. "Always did and then somewhere I lost track of looking for the right one and finding only the one handy. Not a way to raise a family."

She got out of the chair, hearing his tapping. She didn't even think he knew she got close though he didn't flinch when she put a hand on either shoulder, then slowly slid them forward over his chest, leaning into him, his hard muscles under her hands making her breath catch, but just a little.

The typing stopped, he leaned back into the chair and she nuzzled his neck where it met his shoulder.

His hand came up to hold onto her arm.

"I take it you're not going to let me finish this scene?" His voice was thicker, his breath heavier.

"Not if I can help it."

He unlatched her arms and turned the chair to face her, reaching up to put a hand on the back of each thigh. He pulled until she dropped into his lap, her leg bent and braced on either side of his legs, her hands on his chest.

"It's harder to work like this," he said, wrapping a hand around her neck and pulling her forward until his mouth was on hers, his tongue smooth against hers.

When he stopped, he stared at the point on her chest that wasn't indecent.

"I wasn't there for the creation," he said softly.

"I think you might have shown up at least for a few minutes."

He chuckled. "Okay, I'll give you that one." He looked her in the eyes. "But I wasn't allowed to participate in anything else. Doctors' visits, the heartbeat, seeing the ultrasound. I was kept out of everything. Even when he was born, they were supposed to call me so I could be there but they didn't. I didn't know she was in the hospital. It was twelve hours before they remembered."

"I'm sorry," she said, rubbing the back of her fingers on his cheek.

"I think I would have really liked to see all that and get to know him sooner."

"They should have let you be there."

"We probably would have fought and her mom is worse than her. She hated my guts even before I supposedly ruined Elaine's career by ruining her figure." He looked at her. "But it was about him. Not us."

"How can you be so sure? About this. Us. With everything going on?"

"You're not sure?"

"I am right now, but I don't know if this is reality. Maybe I'm using you for protection and I don't know it."

"Maybe you are."

Her gaze dropped. "I feel safe here. I feel safe with you."

"You are," he whispered.

"I don't want to end hurting you because it was all an illusion."

"It's not. I was already here before this all started. Me being here is one of the reasons this did start. I didn't wait when it would've been a better idea."

"That's you."

"It's you, too. You were there, too. You just didn't know it."

"How can you be sure?"

"Because you kissed me back. You didn't ask me to stop. And you didn't push me away. My hands were on you and you didn't seem to mind. In fact, when it was done, you could still look me in the eye and smile shyly. And now you're breaking my legs."

She smiled and then laughed out. Then staring at him she said, "I want to go to bed with you."

His gaze dropped, he drew in a breath and blew it out with pursed lips.

"I have very little self-control with that subject."

"I like how it sounds."

"And it's *so* not easy every night, but I have to say no. I'm not going to do that with this relationship. I did it with too many others. This is different. You and I are different. I have to stand by that." He looked up at her. "The best I can offer is a short date. Couple of weeks maybe put it all together and make it decent."

"Couple of hours and hit the courthouse? You know, all eight of us go in armored vehicles."

He laughed. "You haven't met my mother yet. That would not work. And there is your mother and sisters. Adian—oh forget Adian. He would take the courthouse today."

"Can I make a request?"

"If you get off my legs soon. You're actually not as light as you look."

She couldn't get the words out.

He bobbed his head for a better view. "What?"

"I was thinking we might leave birth control at home."

He put his hand on her chest, between her breasts, only mildly hitting the rise under his palm.

"You're offering?"

His hand, flat against her moved downwards with agonizing slowness. He didn't bring his gaze away from his hand.

"If you're asking," she said.

He leaned back in the chair, his hand on her stomach, deep in thought. He closed his eyes and rubbed his mouth with the same hand that was just on her.

He dropped the hand, opened his eyes and smiled.

"I hope she has your eyes."

Beeman, the gentleman helping them, was excessively patient dealing with the entourage that had graced his Tiffany's showroom on Rodeo Drive in Beverly Hills.

Michael and Kevin were at the door on alert.

Seth at the back.

Allonzo and Scott four feet away and watching everything but the exchange going on in front of them.

Street clothes with large leather coats to hide weapons, Sean knew they all wore vests under their blending in uniform. He knew because Allonzo had made the three of them wear them, too. Even Adian in a small size. Sean had no idea where Allonzo found it.

The biggest annoyance, Sean thought, staring at poor Beeman, had to be the bride-to-be. Sean would bet the odds, not many women walked into this store saying the same things.

"I'm really not into diamonds."

"It's way too showy for what I do."

"Is there something smaller?"

"I understand," Beeman said and smiled in his two thousand dollar suit. "But, for arguments sake, to make Mr. Branigan happy—his mother comes in here, you see—do you prefer white gold? You seem like a white gold person to me."

She nodded and shrugged. "Yeah, I guess. I was never into gold."

"You're not into diamonds, either." Sean smiled.

"Do you like round cut? Princess cut?"

"What are we talking about?"

Sean laughed and leaned forward to look in the case. "How about a round cut. Two carats center weight. More on the sides, and on the band, too. Something, I don't know, with the metal swirling the stones."

Beeman smiled widely. "I see you've done this before."

Sean laughed. "Did you just say you knew my mother?"

Sean smiled at Beth, never having imagined anything could be so fun in their lives right now. Just getting out of the house was a blessing. Sean had to play on Allonzo's mushy side to get him to approve the trip. They drove a two car armored Hummer convoy with armed guards. Sean wasn't sure proposing was supposed to go like this.

He looked at Beeman. "We're going to need a set for her and matching band for me."

"You know you haven't asked," she said.

"Actually I did. I have a witness, but I'll get around to doing it right again."

The rings picked out, sizes taken and credit card used, the group exited the building with talks of where to go to celebrate.

Right outside the door, all hell broke loose when shots blasted directly into the Tiffany's storefront.

Allonzo dove with Adian. Sean moved toward Beth, but was grabbed by Michael and hurled to the ground. Jared shoved Beth down to cover her with his body.

As fast as it started, it was over.

It took a couple more seconds for Kevin to yell clear. Then and only then Sean was allowed to rise and look back and forth to make sure they were both all right.

The window behind them held over a dozen holes in the cracked but not broken safety glass. The smell of gunpowder made the scenario too real.

Kevin still had his gun drawn and ready. Seth, too.

Jared was the last to move, allowing Beth to slide out from under him as he fell back, a red stain on his chest, right this side of the vest.

Beth gasped and jumped back while Adian ran into her embrace. She wrapped her arms around him, pulling his face close, blocking him from seeing.

Michael hit the phone for the ambulance while Kevin went to work administering first aid. Jared was breathing and conscious but Sean stared at him, very aware he had taken a bullet for them.

Very aware, Jared had taken *Beth's* bullet.

Sean looked to Allonzo.

"Answers one question," the dark friend said.

CHAPTER NINE

Two days later, the tension in the house sat raw even with the knowledge that Jared would be fine and back on the job in a few months.

A lot of hugs in the family. A lot of TV—comedies only. A lot of time trying not to talk about Miles Criswell, the situation or how it would finally end.

Sitting in the kitchen with Beth, Sean drank his beer and smiled and forced down the sheer terror that never left. This woman, he thought as he smiled, could be taken away at any second because a nut imagined things that weren't there.

"I don't want it to be like the last book," she said. She had her workbook and some of research books beside her. "I want spooky, maybe a few kisses."

"Your last book was good. Five stars."

"You read it?" she asked, smiling, surprised.

"I read it six months ago. And the one before it. I think you need to get the rest out. And then I think you and I should discuss a division change."

"What do you mean?"

"Ever think of writing scripts?"

"On the show? No."

"Bullshit." He laughed and took a drink.

"What?"

"I found your fan fiction to *Snap Shots* online two years ago. And it was good. Dead on. You nailed the characters and the stories and not once made them do anything weird."

She gasped and then opened her mouth. "You read those?"

He smiled and nodded.

"Those weren't supposed to be read. That was just practice with some ideas. Oh God, you read those?"

"Point of interest? If you don't want them read, don't post them on the Internet."

"That was for the forums. To get feedback."

He was still grinning as he nodded. "I like the name you used. Hardwick69. So much talent and that's the best you could do?"

She punched him in the shoulder. "How did you find out?"

"It was on a fan fic sitting on your desk when I came in once."

She buried her face in her hands but not before he saw her face turning a dark shade of red.

"If you use a name like that, more people will respond," she said.

"Yeah," he smiled. "I'm sure it was your nouns they were after."

Her hands dropped. "Why didn't you offer me the job then?"

"I was probably with someone I shouldn't be and I might have suspected two years ago if I got close I might not be coming back."

"What about now?"

He leaned over and she met him for the kiss. "Now I know I'm not coming back."

"Dad," Adian said, a hitch to his voice catching Sean's attention.

"What's wrong?"

Adian stepped into the room looking shell-shocked.

"I was just on the computer."

"And?"

"On Twitter. They're talking about. It's streaming now and everyone is commenting."

"On what?"

"The studio, Dad. The studio is on fire."

Sean leaned a little forward. "What?"

Allonzo already had the controls for the TV in the kitchen wall and had a news station on. Across the screen two studio newscasters switched feed to Jesse live in the field who wasn't so much concerned with her appearance tonight.

"I can barely hear you, Mark," she said as the wind blew her papers and hair, *"There is so much going on. Helicopters, people. It's a disaster. No one knows the amount of people who have been hurt."*

Behind Jesse, the black night lit up orange, showcasing the building in shadows which were in the fire's path. The flames, thirty feet high, showed no mercy as it took down another recognizable landmark set. The mountains, the trees, all showed black until they ignited.

Jesse spoke but Sean didn't hear. He read the crawl on the bottom, listing the known and suspected damage.

The set of Snap Shots was completely destroyed.

"Dad," Adian whispered, looking scared. Sean opened his arms and his son ran to him, his arms going around Sean's waist, his face in his shirt.

Sean's phone went off. Allonzo's phone, too.

"I know," Sean said into the cell. "I'm watching it."

Allonzo walked into the other room.

"Mack, I can't. You know I can't."

She talked loud enough to be heard in the room. No words. Just voice.

"Go," Beth said.

Sean swore. "Shit."

Allonzo came in, and Sean stared at him, then hung up the phone.

"I can take you," Allonzo said. "In my car."

Sean looked at her. She stared back, now Adian was in her arms.

"Twenty minutes there," Sean said. "Twenty to access, twenty back. I promise."

"Go," she said. "That is a major portion of your life going up in smoke."

"All of which can be replaced."

"We have Michael, we have Seth. One hour."

Beth was walking from the living room to the bedroom with Adian when the one hour became just too long.

Seth took the perimeter on the outside. Michael stayed inside with them.

The front door exploded in bright orange which got hold of the wood and continued burning. Grabbing a throw off the couch, Michael holstered his gun and ran to the door, pulling it open even as he raised the blanket to the flames.

He screamed as his body began to convulse and dance, backing up and letting Miles in, the Taser in Miles hand, the contacts attached to Michaels's chest.

Michael tried to fight it. She could see that, but the charge kept going, until Michael fell to his knees then onto his back, gasping, barely conscious.

Miles tossed the Taser on top of him, pulled a gun from his belt and walked, standing over Michael.

Miles fired a shot into Michael's head.

"Holy shit," she whispered, already backing up, her hand on Adian's chest.

Miles started toward them.

"Flash bomb," he said. "Won't start anything on fire. Well here, anyway. You might have to look for work."

"Go," she whispered to Adian.

But Adian didn't move. She spun and dropped in front of him grabbing him by the shoulders, pushing. "Run. Get outside."

Looking her in the eyes, the rotten child shook his head slightly.

Then Beth was yanked hard and she saw Adian jump back.

Miles spun her to him, backhanding her in the face, blacking out her eyes then dropping her to the floor.

The effort it took was monumental, but the instinct to protect Adian as intact as if he was her own flesh and blood. She pulled herself up and stood as straight as she could. Miles had made it to Adian and her fear burned hot.

"Let him go. Miles. He is not a part of this."

He held Adian by the throat, squeezing so tight Adian's face began to redden. Adian fought back, hitting with closed fists but they only bounced off Miles.

"Yeah, but can you imagine what it would do to Branigan?"

"Can you imagine what it would do to you? He is a child for God's sake. A goddamn child. You could never live with yourself. Not two minutes."

She grabbed a crystal vase from the end table and hurled it, nailing Miles in the back. It shattered but barely fazed him. He dropped Adian and Adian scrambled away while Miles turned toward her.

"You were a great lay," he said. "But you never let on what kind of a bitch you are and certainly never sweet talked me the way you sweet talk him."

"Well we're even," she said backing up, seeing him getting closer. She could try to fight but it wouldn't work. He would take her down like he did in the condo. Her only chance was words. "You never let on you were a psychopath."

He stuck the gun in his belt.

He pulled the switchblade out, snapping it open with drama and she flinched. She could see Adian backing away behind Miles and it was a spark of hope.

"Do you know what I'm going to do to that kid while you watch?"

"If I told you I was pregnant and it wasn't yours, that would really piss you off, wouldn't it?"

His attention shifted from Adian to her.

117

"Leave me, get knocked up by him. Yeah. That might annoy me."

She laughed. "I'm sure it would because every time we did it—and my God it was a lot—it left your pathetic attempts at seduction in the dust. You ever see one of his love scenes? What he does to his leading lady? It is nothing compared to what he does to his leading lady."

Veins popped out on his forehead as his expression turned red.

"I know how to deal with unfaithful bitches like you."

"They were better," she said. "Your heroes. Dahmer. Speck, Bundy. All of them. You're a wanna be with books about men who either got locked up or died for their sins."

"We never talked about those books. I wanted to but you wouldn't have understood."

"You're right." Her back hit the piano and she had nowhere to go. She let out a hard breath feeling the horror in every inch of her body.

And he kept getting closer.

"Wanna know who my favorite was?"

"Not really," she said.

"I like the cutters. I like them up close, feeling the warmth on your fingers until it goes cold. You watch and their eyes go blank. It's beautiful."

"You've done this before?"

He smiled and nodded and he was right in front of her.

"Beg."

"Fuck you is about as good as it gets."

"I think killing you might kill Branigan so bad he never recovers. He's going to know it was his fault. He might as well have killed you himself. He shouldn't have touched what was mine."

Resigned and hating it, she laughed a little. "You fucking moron. I was never yours. You never stood a chance."

His hand snapped up, embedding the blade deep into her side. She gasped at the intense pain, her knees buckling. She grabbed onto his shoulders, holding herself up, sucking in air. She smelled his smoky shirt, his sweat. His eyes so close, she saw the insanity in the bloodshot orbs and kicked herself for never seeing it before.

He shoved on the blade further and her eyes blacked out.

When he yanked it out, it hurt as much as going in.

He put it to her throat, the blade flush and she closed her eyes.

"Open them,"

"No." She could see Sean when they were closed. Adian. The damn cats. She smiled a little thinking it wasn't too bad as a last thought.

He kneed her in the groin which would've doubled her over if he wasn't holding her up. "Then I'll cut your bastard out before I kill the kid. Open them."

She did.

"Get away from my mom," a scared trembling voice said and she closed her eyes tight. He hadn't run. He didn't hide. He would watch her die and then be next. She yanked but couldn't get away.

Miles wrapped his fingers on her throat to hold her steady, the knife still in that hand, and he turned three quarters.

"Put the gun down."

"I said get away from her."

She saw Miles glance at his waistband and the gun and he thought about it.

He let go of her. With the only thing holding her up gone, she fell to her knees.

"Come on kid. It's a big gun." Miles moved two feet to the left while she braced her hands on her knees and looked up with heavy breaths.

"You're not going to hurt my mom. And you're not going to hurt my dad. Not ever."

"What the fuck you going to—"

Adian didn't say another word.

With deadly aim, he fired off four or five shots—she couldn't count—all hitting Miles, making him dance. His hands dropped away, he gurgled and spit and fell face forward on the carpet.

Beth grabbed onto her side with one hand, the table with the other. And pulled herself up.

"Adian. Lower it."

Adian did.

She limped over to the prone Miles, put a finger to his throat and thanked God for miracles. Blood seeped out from the edges, making a pool in the wool.

Adian ran to her, the gun still in hand launching himself into her. Pain shot through her but she wrapped an arm around him, breathing him in.

She held for a minute, and then sunk to her knees. "You have to call 911. Do you understand?"

He fell back, his tear-stained face looking at her.

"You have to do exactly as I say. You can't fudge on anything."

He nodded.

"Call 911. Tell them the guard is down and the intruder is dead. Tell them you need an ambulance. Can you do that?"

He nodded.

"Then go to the kitchen. Use the dish soap and the sponge. I want you to use the green side that hurts, okay? Scrub your hands, your fingers, your arms. Everywhere exposed. Clean up the mess then change your shirt. Throw this one on the fire. Okay? Do you know what to do?"

He nodded.

She put her palm to his face, smiling, leaving a blood mark on him. "Go."

When he was clear, she struggled to move beside Miles' prone body. She pushed and grunted until he flipped and was on his back. Grabbing the gun, she pushed herself up and moved to his feet. Taking aim at the blood and holes already there, she fired two shots into his chest.

"What?" Adian screamed.

"It's okay," she said. "It's me."

She dropped down on to her knees and wiped the gun down with her shirt before putting her hand back on the trigger and butt. Blackness was descending behind her eyelids and her breathes were getting short.

In the kitchen, she heard the water running, then it shut off.

She liked it. She liked it here. She liked it with them. They might have made a real family.

That was her last thought before she fell face down and blacked out.

She woke slowly, fighting consciousness and preferring the dark. There was pain where she was pretty sure there shouldn't be. Her side felt on fire, her insides may have been rearranged.

When her eyes finally opened, Sean was back in his chair, leaning back, his eyes closed, his hands folded over his middle.

This time he really was asleep. She stayed quiet, the IV in her arm, feeling a little loopy from whatever. Her thoughts were coming fuzzy and she didn't know what was real and what was not.

He didn't stay asleep long, jerking awake with an expression saying he wasn't quite sure where he was. His gaze shifted to her, but he didn't smile.

He sat up and rubbed his eyes. He braced his elbows on his knees and put his head in his hands. The silence, too long.

"Seth and Michael are dead," he finally said.

"I knew about Michael. I didn't know about Seth. I'm sorry."

"He was electrocuted on the car. The Audi."

"What?"

"It was wired," Sean said with a shake of his head. "With like eight million volts. Seth brushed up on it or touched it, we don't know. But we're thinking it was not Seth it was meant for. Apparently I was supposed to drive myself to the fire."

His gaze came up to hers, his hands clasped together.

"You know, I know these guys know what they do and the risk is part of it. It always has been and they accept that. Only this time, it was supposed to be me and Seth is supposed to be alive and I have a lot of trouble with it."

"It's not your fault, Sean."

His gaze came up to hers. "He had two kids. I haven't called yet, but I'm going to. I was thinking of setting up a college fund or something. God, I have to do something. His family loses him protecting mine."

"I don't know what to say Sean. It was him. Not you. He did these things. He killed them. Not you."

"Seth is gone. So is Miles, but he did do damage. Took out our set and a large portion of the studio. It will be years before it's back right."

He looked at her.

"You've been out about eighteen hours. A lot of it was surgery. He knew what he was doing and it was close." He looked up at her. "It was way, way too close. Adian stopped some of the bleeding with pressure. Probably made the difference."

"Is Adian okay?"

His gaze came up to hers and the look didn't say good.

"He will be but he might be messed up for a while. We're selling the house. Three bodies, almost four and the fourth we really liked, doesn't really make it cozy anymore."

He said *liked*, past tense. *Past tense*. She sunk back into the pillows and closed her eyes. Emotions ran high not to feel the tears in the corner of her eyes.

"I feel really funky," she said.

"Well, they're pumping you full of all sorts of drugs. Might take a while to adjust. Police are closing the case. It's not official yet but they were here and told me. It will be a few days. They aren't going to pursue anything even with the discrepancies after all the reports we filed."

She wasn't sure she heard him right over the cotton in her ears.

She closed her eyes again. "You said discrepancies?"

She looked at him and he nodded slowly. "There was blood where there shouldn't be blood like on the piano when all the action took place ten feet away. And he had been flipped. Blood stains screamed it."

She looked at the foot of the bed.

"He was shot seven times. Even at the crime scene, it was obvious five shots had come from one angle and two from another. Police noticed and decided not to pursue."

She looked down again, wanting a way out while he stared at her.

"He told you," she whispered.

"Of course he told me. Question is—were you going to?"

"I don't know. I was there and then here and nothing in between. I haven't had any time to think. And right now, thinking is hard. Fuzzy."

He kept on looking at her.

"I don't know. Probably. It would have been hard, but it's kinda too big a secret to keep. So yeah, I guess."

He nodded. "Why two shots?"

"Gunshot residue. I wanted it off him and on me. I didn't want anyone going after him. I tried to get the same angle, but it was hard."

"I bet it was. And it worked. You were checked after surgery and you tested positive."

"Did they check him?"

Sean shook his head. "No. The world thinks you killed Miles Criswell."

"Is Adian okay?"

"It was Michael's gun," he said. "My son went to his dead friend and got his gun to stop the assault. I don't want him to have seen that. To see Michael like that, but Adian did good. He's shaken up and we'll be calling doctors who don't talk. He doesn't want to be alone. He's got Allonzo with him right now and we're heading for a beach house for a month or so."

"Did Miles hurt the cats?"

Sean smiled a little and shook his head. "They hid, but came out. They're on their way to Malibu."

"I did it to protect him, Sean."

"You think I don't know that? He told me everything you did. Wanted to know about the baby, only I know for a fact what you said wasn't true and the hospital did run a routine test so I know Criswell didn't leave anything behind."

"What are you talking about?" Her voice was breathless.

"You don't remember?"

She shook her head and then "No I don't...wait..."

He waited.

"Yeah, I do. I said it to piss Miles off. He had Adian. I had to get him off Adian and figured that would be it."

"He was going to kill you for it."

"But Adian had a chance."

"You were willing to die to save my son." He shook his head and rubbed his face. "I don't think his biological mother would do that."

"You've never called her that before."

He dropped his hands, raised his eyes and smiled. "I had to find a way to distinguish. Adian won't call you anything but mom now so we're having to adapt."

She looked at him and felt a tear fall. "I kinda got the feeling you didn't want me anymore."

"Because you saved my son? You think I don't want you because you saved my son?"

"I brought this to you."

He looked down and laughed a little. "Honey, I kissed you. Technically I started it."

He leaned back in his chair, closed his eyes tight and uttered, "Oh crap."

She sighed at that and then heard the footsteps in the hall he must have already heard.

The woman who walked into the room was as breathtaking in her seventies as she had been in her twenties and thirties. Beth had seen her films and having the legend in the room sucked the air out of her lungs.

Barbara Swenson. Three time Academy Award Nominee, one time winner. Two Golden Globes. A couple of Tonys. And a lot more that lined her shelves but what they were for weren't in Beth's head right now.

Barbara's grey hair, swept back was as magnificent as when it had been dark, when she was younger. Her pale blue blouse, a match for the eyes, clothed a figure that still looked beautiful. There were large diamonds at her ears, on her wrist and two diamond rings on her fingers.

Sean smiled wide as the older woman batted him on the back of the head.

"You said you would call me when she woke up."

He flinched only a little and it was more humor than anything.

He raised his arm, his elbow on the chair arm and pointed up, like he was making a point.

"Beth, this is *Mommm*."

"Yeah," she sighed. "I know."

"He's always been sort of a dolt on these things," Barbara said.

She pulled a tissue out of the box. "Oh you poor thing. This was too much, even in our family." She dabbed at Beth's face. She touched the side of Beth's swollen cheek, where Miles hit her. "We can fix that," Barbara smiled. "I know lots of tricks."

She stood up straight. "He's got terrible taste in women, too. Always has."

"Mom," he groaned.

"His first was in junior high and even she was a skank. But then her mother was…" she thought better of it. "Well her mother was on a show. Not a good one, either. No morals in that family."

"Mom, I will get the duct tape. I swear to God I will get the duct tape."

"Adian tells me you're different from all the rest. You're smart, Adian says, and you can outthink this one." She nodded toward Sean. "You're a writer and reader and you love cats."

His mom turned to scowl at him. "Did any of your other girlfriends love cats?"

"All of them. Every single one of them. They were crazy cat ladies in hiding—can you shut up now?"

"I checked it out," she said.

"Oh God," Sean moaned. "Timing?"

She looked at him. "Timing is perfect. She needs cheering up and these were your plans all along, right?"

"So not the point, Mom."

She turned back to the overwhelmed Beth.

"I think I need more drugs," Beth said.

Sean laughed. "How do you think we got through puberty?"

"I checked the Bay area," Barbara said, "but it seems it might be far with your mom."

"My mom?"

"For the wedding. I don't want to tax her in traveling so we will arrange something easy."

"Wedding?"

Sean was rubbing the side of his face, he looked up at Beth. "She likes to plan things."

"So I thought The Bay might be too far. And then I had this idea."

"Of course you did."

"The Queen Mary in Long Beach. It has a gorgeous chapel, very intimate with the old Hollywood charm. Cary Grant and Bob Hope used to travel on the Queen Mary. We can rent out the whole thing and have a small ceremony with only our closest."

"You're going to invite Dad?" Sean asked and chuckled.

She turned to glare at him then looked back to Beth.

"And then we rent a boat—"

"She means a yacht."

"What?" Beth gasped.

"Then you two take off for a week or two in Avalon, I'll take Adian. Will your father be at the ceremony?"

"He died when I was sixteen."

"I am so sorry."

Beth was sure she meant it. Her hand on Beth's was warm.

"That is too young to lose a parent. Well, Sean has two brothers. You can choose one of them to give you away and let the other think you have a favorite."

"It was fun growing up in my house," Sean chuckled.

"I have everything booked with deposits so all we need to do is get you healthy and find the right outfits for everyone. I know a perfect place to get your dress and then December 24th we gather."

"The 24th?"

"Yes", Barbara smiled. "Christmas Eve. I thought after all this, it would be the perfect Christmas present for you two. The new Mr. and Mrs. Sean and Beth Branigan."

He looked right at Beth. "I told you," he said. "I told you a long time ago. There will never be a way out."

ABOUT THE AUTHOR

Award-winning author, Jacqui Jacoby lives and writes in the beauty of Northern Arizona. Currently adjusting to being an empty nester with her first grandchild to draw her pictures, Jacqui is a self-defense hobbyist. Having studied martial arts for numerous years she retired in 2006 from the sport, yet still brings strength she learned from the discipline to her characters. She is a working writer, whose career includes writing books, novellas & short stories, teaching online & live workshops and penning short nonfiction.

Follow her at www. jacquijaxjacoby.com

http://jaxsmovielist.blogspot.com/

Twitter: JaxJacoby

Facebook: Jacqui Jax Jacoby

Google + Jacqui Jacoby

Instagram: JacquiJaxJacoby

ALSO BY JACQUI JACOBY

NOW AVAILABLE

With a Vengeance

Dead Men Play the Game

Magic Man

COMING SOON

Dead Men Seal the Deal, available February 2016

Illegal Exit: a novella, available May 2016

The Dead Men, A Collections of Twelve Short Stories,

available August, 2016

Illegal Exit—a novella

© 2016 Jacqui Jacoby, Body Count Productions, Inc

Available May, 2016

Sitting in the jump seat of a van with mesh covered windows, Trevor Martin let them buckle him in, thinking about how much he truly hated the color orange.

If he had a chance, it would be the last color he ever put on his body again.

"Why the transfer?" He asked the guard across from him. The driver stared at the road, the guard in front didn't turn around.

"Because of shut the fuck up."

"Clever," Trevor smiled. "Can I know where I have to go at two o'clock in the morning? No one told me about this."

"Is there a part of what I said that you didn't understand?"

Trevor closed his eyes and let his head fall back.

Over five years ago everything that was normal died. Trevor became a man he didn't know he was. He did things he didn't know he could and never regretted them. Not even when he was caught, arrested, and tossed in a little cell by himself.

Tried with his cousin, Gavin, they were kept apart since the verdict was read. They not only lost everyone else, they lost each other when each other was all they had. Raised as brothers who had shared everything from toys, to jeans, to date stories, now they were sharing one more thing.

They were going away for life.

They were never going to see each other again.

The van pulled into a darkened lot near a wired and barbed fence. Trevor, with his back to the door, didn't know it was Gavin loaded in, until Gavin had been secured across from him. He looked as shocked as Trevor felt.

It had been four months since they had sat at the table with their lawyers and Gavin looked good. Thinner, but good. Even in orange.

They stared at each other.

"Any clue?"

Trevor thinned his lips tight and shook his head.

"Great," Gavin sighed, looking to the side. "So not good."

They drove for two hours in a silence as total as any they had ever experienced.

The terrain changed from city to rural until the van started up into the hills. Probably easier to throw the body in a ditch in the middle of nowhere, Trevor thought.

New Jersey didn't have the death penalty. At least not before now.

He thought of them. The names he never dared think of.

Mom. Aunt Lucy. Emily. Jayce. Caleb. Sarah. Baby Lucas.

All sharing a gravesite at Centuries Eternal. Mom had been forty-two. Lucas was eighteen months. Everyone else in between.

Trevor looked at Gavin.

"Remember the last Christmas?"

Gavin smiled and nodded his head. "Mom tried that turkey she got on discount."

"Piece of leather with wings," Trevor laughed. "God, it was awful."

"Hey, shut the fuck up back there."

"Why?" Trevor snapped. "Harder to shoot us in here than out there?"

The guard had his hand on his gun, but backed down.

"You never told her," Gavin said.

"She tried so hard and was so proud. I couldn't take that from her and you should talk. You had seconds."

They both, shackled to the floor, laughed hard.

"Regrets?" Trevor asked.

Gavin looked to the back of the van and then at Trevor, his chin tilted to smile.

"I still think we should have gone to IHOP."

They were arrested in a Denny's. Trevor smiled as the van pulled off and took a dirt road.

The van stopped in a clearing and the lights switched off.

www.ingramcontent.com/pod-product-compliance
Lightning Source LLC
Chambersburg PA
CBHW020247150626
46552CB00020B/636